THE DAY THE HORSES WENT TO THE FAIR

ANIMAL LOVER AND PAINTER: ROSA BONHEUR

A SINGULAR NOVEL

NORMAN BEAUPRÉ

For Lois and Christine, dear friends

Je vous apporte BONHEUR

WORKS BY THE SAME AUTHOR :

1. *L'Enclume et le couteau, The Life and Works of Adelard Coté, Folk Artist,* Photos by Stephen Muskie, NMDC, Manchester, N.H., 1982. Reprint by Llumina Press, Coral Springs, FL. 2007.

2. *Le Petit Mangeur de Fleurs,* Éd. JCL, Chicoutimi, Québec, 1999.

3. *Lumineau,* Éd. JCL, Chicoutimi, Québec, 2002.

4. *Marginal Enemies,* Llumina Press, Coral Springs, FL, 2004.

5. *Deux Femmes, Deux Rêves,* Llumina Press, Coral Springs, FL. 2005.

6. *La Souillonne, Monologue sur scène,* Llumina Press, Coral Springs, FL. 2006.

7. *Before All Dignity Is Lost,* Llumina Press, Coral Springs, FL. 2006.

8. *Trails Within, Meditations on the Walking Trails at the Ghost Ranch in Abiquiu, New Mexico,* Llumina Press, Coral Springs, FL. 2007.

9. *La Souillonne deusse,* Llumina Press, Coral Springs, FL. 2008.

10. *The Boy With the Blue Cap---Van Gogh in Arles,* Llumina Press, Coral Springs, FL. 2008.

11. *Voix Francophones de chez nous---contes et histoires* par Normand Beaupré et autres, Llumina Press, Coral Springs, FL, 2009.

12. *La Souillonne, Dramatic Monologue,* translated from French by the author, Llumina Press, Coral Springs, FL. 2009.

13. *The Man With the Easel of Horn----the Life and Works of ÉMILE FRIANT,* Llumina Press, Coral Springs, FL. 2010.

14. *The Little Eater of Bleeding Hearts* translated from French, *Le Petit Mangeur de Fleurs,* by the author, Llumina Press, Coral Springs, FL. 2010.

15. *Simplicity in the Life of the Gospels, Spiritual Reflections*, Llumina Press, Coral Springs, FL. 2011.

16. *Madame Athanase T. Brindamour, raconteuse, histoires et folleries*, Llumina Press, Coral Springs, FL. 2012.

17. *Cajetan the Stargazer*, Llumina Press, Coral Springs, FL. 2012.

18. *L'Étranger Extraterrestre*, Llumina Press, Coral Springs, FL, 2013.

19. *Marie-Quat'e-Poches et Sarah Foshay----Dialogue à Deux Faces*, Llumina Press, Coral Springs, FL. 2013.

20. *The Fallen Divina---Maria Callas*, Llumina Press, Plantation, FL, 2015

21. *Souvenances d'une Enfance Francophone Rêveuse*, Llumina Press, Plantation, FL, 2016.

PREFACE

have loved writing about artists, makers and smithies of fine arts, and weaving threads of the imagination throughout the entire tapestry of my work. So far, I have written two novels based on the lives and works of two French artists: Vincent Van Gogh and Émile Friant. I enjoyed writing these novels since they both stirred my imagination and my creativity in writing about painters and their paintings. Paintings offer the opportunity of detailing each work with words and using my imagination in recreating each stroke of the brush and each daub of paint that the artist uses. I try to put myself in the shoes of the artist as he struggles, at times, to put on canvas what he sees in his mind's eye while duplicating his model before him. I try to envision texture, harmony of color, scope of perspective, and faithfulness to light and color. Choosing the right words is a matter of selecting words that effectively bring out the sense of artistry on the part of the artist at work either in a field of blossoms or indoors gazing at his subject. For me, words must bring out the richness of color and light, and they have to be suggestive so as to bring in the reader into my realm of using all of the five senses to prevail on my choice of words. In other words, they must convey exactly or at least approximately well the shapes and the colors highlighted by luminosity that appear before me as I assess the composition before my very eyes. The artist creates his art with his own skill of painting while I create my art as a writer by selecting words and putting them into phrases and sentences that will convey the exactitude of seeing with my mind's eye what the artist has done in creating his work of art. Of course, in order to keep verisimilitude in tow, I attach to the descriptions that I give some of the historical and biographical facts associated with the artist about whom I'm writing. This gives my work a semblance of reality and at the same time a story with which the reader can use his own imagination in attempting to create in her own mind the plot of the story and the descriptions of the paintings that are being presented to her. It's all about creativity, the creativity of the artist, the creativity of the writer and the creativity of the reader, all in synchronous movements like a symphony. How often have I heard from one of my readers that what I had written about a particular work of art imitated very well the actual painting and rendered faithfully the exact tone of color, light and shapes of the painting they were looking at in order to see what I had written was actually the painting they were looking at. When there are no illustrations available in the novel, the reader must search out the illustration of the painting in question. This gives the reader an opportunity to thumb through some of the books of illustrations of the works of a given artist. This is my way of stimulating the reader to get into the life of the works of art that will not only stimulate her but also give her a feeling for the fine arts. I'm still very much the teacher at heart after thirty plus years of trying to involve students with creativity. The power of the brush and the power of the word are such that they can change someone's life by uncovering the often latent power of receptivity in the viewer and the reader. I'm convinced of that.

Upon seeing Rosa Bonheur's huge painting of the horses at the Paris fair, almost taking up an entire wall at the Metropolitan Museum of Art in New York, I stood there in amazement and awe. I could not move a muscle so fascinated was I with this astonishing work of art. I had read about it, but I had never once seen the actual painting. It is at that moment that I decided to write a novel on Rosa Bonheur and her works of art dealing principally, if not exclusively, with animals. Besides, I wanted to include women artists in my writing of novels about painters of the past. Rosa Bonheur was indeed a fine choice since it led me to reading more and more about her life and her works. It's a challenge that I have enjoyed before and that I accepted with the satisfying joy of an author finding the subject of his next book. I trust the reader will understand and become eager to start the reading. Let the creative process begin.

CHAPTER ONE

For some who know me and my work, I need no introduction, but for those who do not know me and my paintings, I need to let them know that I'm a well-known French painter of the 19th Century and was known as an *animalière,* a painter of animals or, as some would say, a wildlife painter. I loved animals and my entire life was filled with them. I enjoyed them and they were my constant companions, especially when I lived in the Chateau de By next to Fontainebleau. How I loved the forest of Fontainebleau and its vast expanse of trees and wild life. You could say that my dreams and my thoughts were ever haunted by animals. I sought to bring them to life in my paintings, and that is why I am known as a realist painter.

My name is Rosa Bonheur. I was born in Bordeaux although I moved with my family to Paris then to other locations, but my real home, my stable and joy-filled *endroit de créativité* has always been the Chateau de By, near Fontainebleau. Yes, it was truly my creative space. As I am standing here in front of my masterpiece "The Horse Fair", yes, that's the way people and critics see this magnificent painting of horses, I cannot forget how I had offered this huge painting, a quality piece of fine arts, to the Bordeaux officials, my native city, and they refused to purchase it, even at a very special low price that I gave them. What a shame, I thought then as I do now. To this day, Bordeaux has no major work of art of Rosa Bonheur. After all, I am one of them, the Bordelais. The entire thing was so narrow-minded and pinch-Penney of them.

"Horse Fair" came to me as in a vision, although I had had it in my creative mind for quite some time. I loved the fairs where the *Percherons,* that rugged breed of agile draft horses, were often exhibited. I've always loved their strength and their agility. These horses originated in the former Perche province. They were used for forestry work and pulling carriages. In Britain, they were used in the British riding discipline competition. The head of the *Percheron* has a straight profile, broad forehead, large eyes and small ears. The chest is deep and wide and the croup long and level. The overall impression of the *Percheron* is one of power and ruggedness. Theirs is a proud breed, an alert breed. And, I might add that they were considered to be intelligent, willing workers with a good disposition. It's no wonder that they were liked by many who owned them and handled them. I always loved them since they made a fine figure of a horse as compared to the more refined breeds, as they are called. I was never in the horse racing business and never frequented the horse races. I thought that those poor animals were often abused and used for money and gambling. I did not like that.

You may be wondering why I am here at the Metropolitan Museum of Art in New York and how I got here in the 21st Century, so many years after my bones lay under the Micas vault at the Père Lachaise Cemetery. Well, you could say that I am a *revenante,* as they say in French, a ghost of some sorts. I so wanted to have people know me and my paintings all through my lifetime, and never achieved the full results I desired to attain, even though I was never one to go after fame and fortune. I simply wanted to live comfortably in my Chateau de By with my dear friend Anna Klumpke and continue my work as an animal painter. However, an artist needs some recognition now and then, recognition that what she is doing is acknowledged as art, creative art. I always knew that my work was art creatively done and with a sense of knowledge of what I was doing. Not only a sense of knowledge but a sense of well-defined artistry. I knew my subject matter, I knew my colors and I even knew my paintbrushes. They had to be the finest of brushes and clean too. And so, I was given the chance to come back to earth for a short while and promote my work, for the Good Muse of art and creativity wants it so. She lives among the spheres and intercedes for artists like me. People on earth do not see me in the flesh I once had, but my soul is there and I can communicate to those who need my commentaries on art, my art. And I am grateful to the agile mind and heart of my interpreter, the author of this novel, although this is not purely a novel, but I accept that. A novel uses the creative imagination to spin its tale, so to speak. I agree that the creative imagination is being used to put together the fabric of this novel, but I assure you that the work, as a whole, is based on facts and history of my life and my work as well as the quality and realistic dimensions of my paintings. I think I will be very pleased with it. All in all, it's a challenge to my interpreter-novelist. I trust he welcomes a challenge as I have always done during my lifetime. Challenges are the marrow of creativity.

Now for "Horse Fair" or *Marché aux chevaux* as it is known in French, is a huge artistic composition, 244.5 x 506.7 cm if my memory serves me right. It is enormous and takes pretty much of an entire wall here at the Metropolitan thanks to Cornelius Vanderbilt who donated this painting to the museum. I must say that he had an extraordinary eye for good art. The painting was sold to a Samuel Avery acting on behalf of Mister Vanderbilt. If I remember well, it was sold for 250,000 francs. I did not get all of that, but I was pleased with what I did receive. I never wanted to be rich and live in opulence. Never. I worked very hard at this painting that I conceived one day thinking about horses. I put in hours, days, months and even the better part of two years. I was so fascinated with this work that it consumed me. I did sketch after sketch after sketch. Perfection is never attained, but I was close to it. I had to let go at one point for I would have never been totally satisfied with this monumental artistic project.

The painting consists of several horses; it's hard to count them if you're trying to distinguish all of them. There are some dark ones and some gray ones. The gray ones are in the forefront. The focus is essentially on one large gray horse that appears to be of a dazzling white due to the sun's rays. His front legs are up in the air rearing defiantly, and a man holds on to him by the reins, or what appears to be reins. Another horse, this one black, joins in the fray it seems. At least, most people's attention is on this horse and so was mine. However, I did not lend my entire attention to these particular horses since this was a horse fair, and so many animals participated in it. I had to choose some and those that I selected were the ones that truly interested me. You can see that these horses are Percherons and their stunning brawny muscles ripple under their glossy hides. I could not help but to admire them in their full vigor as Percherons.

Their powerful legs and long necks are astonishingly fluid and graceful for such huge animals. I could not help but to admire them as I looked at them and remembered them in my many sketches. I did so many sketches of these horses not just on a particular day but at least twice a week when I went to the horse market place on the tree-lined boulevard de l'Hôpital near the Pitié-Salpêtrière Hospital. You can see it in the background on the left of the painting. There was a raucous and almost unbearably tense atmosphere of the place, and the enthralled spectator of this painting can almost hear the thunder of the great horses' hooves, their neighing mixed with their handler's shouts. Oh, it was a noisy place full of excitement and raw nerves that I remember so very well.

I must admit that the "Horse Fair" derives in part from inspiration of the Parthenon frieze, and that the romantic and flamboyant horses of Théodore Géricault have served as a model for me, although his flair for romantic renditions is a bit too splashy in color and in appearance and too unrealistic for my taste. However, I must admit that Géricault was a master of color and movement. I guess some people would accuse me of being too scientific in my approach to art. I like reality and preciseness, the actual precision of limbs and muscles, heads and eyes as well as the movement of animals. The anatomy of an animal cannot be hidden in the brushstrokes of a painter who has not studied anatomy. I have always focused on such precision and I trust my sense of realism when it comes to painting animals. I like anatomical precision, the rendering of eye contact between an animal and its painter or gazer, the developing relationship between an animal and a human being, and especially the honesty that comes out of such a relationship. Animals sense that and they do not accept a lack of transparency of feelings and a lack of honesty between them and the other, especially human beings. I spent a lot of time studying animals and their response to my efforts to get to know them, really know them and understand them in their own environment. Why, people recognize that I had my very own menagerie and that I relished the closeness between the animals and myself that existed. Animals have feelings too, in some way. They are not simply robots or things to have around as pets of pleasure. My lions were not my pets; they were my loved ones and they loved me in return. I was so close to them especially my lioness, Fathma, but that comes later when you will hear described the painting I made of her.

I must tell you that I studied animal anatomy and osteology by visiting the abattoirs of Paris and by performing dissections of animals at the École nationale vétérinaire d'Alfort, the National Veterinary Institute in Paris. I prepared detailed studies which would later serve me well as references. During this period of my life, I also met and became friends with the father and son, the comparative anatomists and zoologists Étienne Geoffroy Saint-Hilaire and Isidore Geoffroy Saint-Hilaire by whom my father was employed to create natural history illustrations. I truly enjoyed their company and their expertise. I thought them to be artists-scientists. They taught me how to study the muscles, sinews, bones, and even tissues of animals, so that I could not only see the outside of animals but their inner structures. It was fascinating. And, I must admit that through my father's creativity and art with natural history, I learned to become involved with his craft as an artist. That and my studies refined my skills as an artist *animalière.* Call me what you want, but I truly enjoyed what I was doing and what I planned to do with my future. I wanted to paint animals. It's that simple and I did it.

Coming back to this painting before us, take a good look at the movements of the horses and their strong features as draught animals. First, there's the man sitting on one of the gray horses in the forefront holding on to some rope tied to the horses. He is looking the other way, and we can see his strong muscular arms as the sleeves of his white shirt are rolled up. I wanted to show the features of this strong and muscular groom while not revealing his face. His body movements are in synchronization with the movement of the horses he is holding on to. His white shirt strikingly matches the bright light on the gray horse making it pratically white in appearance.

Behind him yet another man in a white shirt, ruddy complexion, mustache and short beard, is holding on to the rope of yet another gray muscular horse. The right eye of this horse is defiant and fiery, his front legs lifted up in muscular supplication to let go. Another man dressed in a blue smock and black cap sits quietly on a brown horse holding the reins as he and his horse are a foil to the fugue of the other horses shared by the men trying to hold on to them.

A bit further down there's a black horse in full fury, it seems, his eyes aflame and his front legs held high in defiance of the flow of things, as yet another man in a blue smock is attempting to grasp the black flowing mane. The horse looks as if he's in utter rage, defiant at the rush of men and horses. This is all part of the dynamic scene I wanted to create, and did so with utter abandon while mastering my art and skill as an artist sifting through the reality of the scene in my mind. There are more men in the thick of things, one with a full mustache, hat on his head, white shirt, wearing a vest and a scarf around his neck, and masterly riding a gray horse. Yet another man standing to the left is walking, holding on to some kind of a makeshift bridle of a brown Percheron seemingly trotting. The man has a white shirt and a vest both wide open at the chest showing the virility of the horse handler. He has the features of what I would call *gitan*, gypsy. Further to the right, is yet another man wearing a cap and a blue smock riding a gray horse, all part of the foray. Yet, still further from the forefront stands a younger man holding on to the bridle of yet another gray horse. We can see the back of his white shirt and the straps holding up his pants. If you look back into the forefront, now you can see the heads of several other men mingled with the heads of other horses. To the very right sits a rider in a blue smock sitting on a brown horse seemingly trotting or forging ahead of the pack. Several other men standing on a small hill up front are watching the rounding of the horses as if this was a show of some kind, a very fascinating show, I might add. That's what I wanted to do with this painting, reveal the ardor, strength, forcefulness and male steadfastness as well as the same qualities and virtues of these Percherons that were being brought to the fair. I wanted dynamism and animal rigor in the men as well as the animal vigor that these beautiful creatures, the Percherons, possess. It's a real scene of horses being led to a real market in Paris. The entire scene is of dynamic turbulence, for a lack of better words. There is movement here, *de l'agitation*, and you can feel it in your fingertips, in your head and even in your responsive guts. Men and horses, Percherons and men excercising animal strength and vigor. At least, that's the way I sensed it, and I may be a bit too subjective about it when I present you the details of this painting. It's a magnificent canvas of men at work with tremendously strong horses on a bright sunny morning in Paris. I have to admit that I truly love this painting for its forcefulness and its realism.

It's a dynamic realism this painting is. It is not at all passive and soulless. However it may be, that's the way the public and the critics reacted to this painting, with enthusiasm and enchantment. That's the way I see it too.

As far as the background is concerned, there are the trees, the cloud-bearing sky and the light and shadows with the faint outline of the cupola of the *Hôpital Salpêtrière* nearby in the pinkish sky way to the left. Even the brownish soil of pebbles and rough indentations reveal the light and shadows that foster the light to spring through the entire painting. The rhythmic disposition of massed horses is the testimony, I strongly believe, of my determined effort of learning hour by hour, day by day through the hundreds of sketches and especially through my observations that came from a keen, ardent and truthfilled eye measured in a scientific way so as to render the realism, if not the majesty, of a dynamic scene that took all of my artistic efforts to conceive and execute. That may sound pompous, but it's the truth. Art is never pompous; it's rightfully transparent and frank.

I was so very proud of this painting when I finished it. I realized that it was a huge canvas and had taken so much energy from me and demanded all of my strength as a woman inspired and determined to succeed in a world so oftentimes dominated by men especially in the field of fine arts. The Géricaults, the Delacroix, the Rembrandts, and all of the proclaimed Impressionists around me, the so-called masters were flaunted and ruled as kings of the art world. I did not want to compete with anyone, any particular artist, but to show everyone that a woman could accomplish what some men had done, and probably even surpass them. It wasn't rivalry but persistence in revealing my strengths and powerful insights into the world of art through the lenses of an animal lover, *une animalière,* if you so want to call me and my art. I was so satisfied and pleased that the Salon of 1853 proved my prowess and extraordinary skill as a painter, and I received much acclaim so that I was able to not so much sit on my laurels but revel in them as an accomplished artist. It feels good as an artist to realize finally that one has arrived and has the power of dauntingly forge ahead into the art world. Not that I wanted to dominate and crow over my success as celebrated in the painting of the "Horse Fair" but I was proud of myself and my work. It took years of *apprentissage* and so much effort in learning details after details of color, light, shadows, and especially of animal fur and animal eyes as well as the sublime movements of each and every animal that I studied from up close, because I not only enjoyed them but I truly got to love them.

I was stunned to acknowledge the acclaim of the public as well as the critics' warm acceptance of my work, this huge canvas that portrayed *le marché aux chevaux* and all its clamor and dynamic animal forcefulness. Even Queen Victoria of England loved this painting and became one of my enthusiastc admirers. I had a special and private showing just for her. I was impressed by her candor and her love of art. Furthermore, Emperor Napoleon III and his wife, the lovely Empress Eugénie, came to the Salon to admire "Horse Fair" although the Emperor did not appreciate Courbet's nude on exhibit there, I was told. The painting travelled from city to city and I received many appreciable comments about this work. Why it did not stay in France is a question of money and a lack of true appreciation of the worth of art and the people who make the decisions to buy and sell artworks. Why Bordeaux refused this painting at an exceptionally low price, I will never know. They did not recognize the value of realistic art and the worth of a painting that showed itself to be a slice of life in Paris with real men and real animals living out a scene of the Parisian marketplace. I suppose that they ever did regret their lack of respectful acknowledgment of one of their own. Only when the painting had become a wonder in the art world did Bordeaux realize it had failed to recognize a masterpiece. To be here and be able to look at the beautiful "Horse Fair" right here at the Metropolitan Museum of Art in New York City is a wonder for me, and certainly not a disappointment. The Americans deserve to have it since it was here that my work was to be enshrined in a spectacular way so that many people might come to view it and admire my art. I know that this museum will never part with it and that more and more people will come and stare at the "Horse Fair" and wonder who that woman was who painted such a masterpiece of dynamic strength, forceful enthusiasm, colorful delight, and realistic intent. *C'est moi!* I would tell them, *moi, Rosa Bonheur.* I was the woman who dared to wear pants...and there's a reason behind it...that I will share with you who want to listen to my story and everything that is part of my story of living and painting although I am not ready to share all of my innermost thoughts and feelings. I have a private life, I'll have you know, and that's why I chose to live and work at Chateau de By away from the eyes and ears of people who wanted to intrude my privacy. That's one of the reasons I loved animals since they did not intrude into my life but rather fulfilled it.

CHAPTER TWO

ow I want to go back into my life as a youngster in Bordeaux and then on to other vicinities where I grew up. The word "tomboy", *garçon manqué* as it is said in French, was not really known to the inhabitants of Bordeaux in the early part of the 19th Century, although certain people knew of girls acting like boys and imitating their gestures and their tomfoolery. They were classified as odd, not too amiable and definitely not lady-like. A lady was a lady and she wore her manners, not on her sleeve, but in her heart as well as in her head, and her behavior was the reflection of the good manners invariably impeccable. Why, she had been trained by those who took care that she was formed that way and educated so that her entire sophistication of manners and style was deeply ingrained in her and was to last way into maturity and even beyond. Any slips of behavior were due to some unwanted but tenuous revolt of the mind against the heart which guided her to be submissive and obedient to those to whom she owed allegiance and faithfulness. Sometimes it wasn't meant to be revolt but simply a kind of knee-jerk reaction to the norms of a society often too demanding of a child growing up. Some children never questioned these norms and simply followed them unreservedly. Others, although there were few especially in the higher stratas of that society that questioned everything and everyone as to why they had to submit to such norms. They were thought to be rebellious if not downright disrespectful of authority. These children just simply could not understand the intractibility of norms and standards be they of men, women, the clergy, or even the authority. They knew that there had to be order in society but why such a rigid code of behavior? It was all under the standard of one precious concept: decorum. Decorum was the means of inflicting upon people and even children what was considered propriety and good taste as the measure of approved behavior. Why make little children become robots of norms, young people angry with themselves and the so-called system, and grown-ups disciplinarians of questionable motives and judgment. Why? I simply hated it when my father often scolded me for being boyish, strong-minded and outspoken. What was wrong with that, I told him. Why was he insisting that I play the stereotypical role of a lady? What or who was a lady anyhow? A woman of culture and delicate hands with a taste for fine things? I was not born to carry on the stereotypes invented by men. Anyhow, I was me, myself, a woman growing into an artist by virtue not of her delicate quality of refinement or savoir-faire, but for her own talents and strength of character. That's the way I saw it.

The Bonheur family in Bordeaux had talent and exercised them. Why, we, the Bonheur family, indulged in and shared the high norms of art and its practice. Father, mother, sons and daughters, all were captivated by the creativity of fine arts. My father, Raimond, was an admired artist who devoted his life to art and especially the social movement known as Saint-Simonianism. He had his own life to live, but it was my mother that I sympathized with the most. Poor Sophie, poor abandoned soul. Most of the time she was alone with we, the four children, and did her best to pull it all together without too much assistance from my father who was away toiling in his social mission wanting to convert the world and add to the followers of this soul-entrenching cult . My mother had a very hard time with this marriage of a cast off princess and a roaming painter who had ideals that did not match his real responsibilities.

Poor mother, poor Sophie, realized that she was the illegitimate fruit of a liaison conducted among expatriate aristocrats during the turbulent years of the French Revolution. She was born near Hamburg, Gemany and raised in Bordeaux by an affluent blue-blooded merchant. My father, Raimond and my mother, Sophie were an obvious misalliance. I recall the grievous discrepancy between my mother's lonely hardship and my father's sublime enthusiasm for the cult that was Saint-Simonianism. My mother, the most noble and proud of creatures, succumbing to exhaustion and wretched poverty while my father was dreaming about saving the human race. My father returned home after the government indicted the leaders. Father then lamented in front of my mother that he had understood too late why celibacy was so necessary to his social calling. My mother cried tears of despair ever so often. She died young at the age of 36, totally exhausted and worn out. Unfortunately, my mother died a pauper's death and was thrown with other poor souls into a potter's field. I will never forgive my father for that. Nourished by the memory of my mother's love, my deep grief over her loss sublimated over time into the conviction that my mother's soul protected, guided, and inspired me throughout my entire life. I will ever treasure the great gift my mother gave me when I was very young trying to learn to read and write. She taught me by having me select and draw an animal for each letter of the alphabet. That was truly fun for me and I learned easily enough. I learned to love letters and animals, and I discovered for myself that I had talent for drawing. Animals were a key point in my learning not only the alphabet but learning about myself as a budding *animalière* .

After my mother's death, my father apprenticed me to a seamstress, an ordinary and desperate fate for a working-class girl in the 19th Century. After I had proven unwiling and inept in that trade, I was expelled from a girls' boarding school. This led to me being placed here and there with people I did not really like, and who did not understand me. In his drive to transform me from une *garçonière,* as he called me, he desperately wanted me to become more lady-like and refined like the other young ladies around me. I wanted to be who I was and I fought him all the way. He then decided to take my education upon himself and taught me how to paint. He had already recognized my talent for drawing and eventually for my copying masterpieces. That was the day when he decided to bring me to the Louvre, this sanctuary of great art, as I called it. It was there that I fell in love with the works of some of the renowned painters that I admired such as, Nicholas Poussin, Peter Paul Rubens, Paulus Potter, Léopold Robert, Salvator Rosa, and Karel Dujardin. I had already copied images from drawing books and made studies of domesticated animals from life: horses, sheep, cows, goats, rabbits and other animals in the pastures on the perimeter of Paris and, of course, in my many walks through the Bois de Boulogne. These woods enchanted me and I never grew tired of going there to observe the trees, the birds, the flowers and the animals that lived there. That was my life, my great desire to live in a forest where the natural kingdom existed and where I belonged as an artist. I so often skipped school just to be in the Bois de Boulogne and enjoy the freedom of being there in the open air.

While at the Louvre I copied the paintings of masters as I have indicated, and for that I earned money enough to supplement my father's income which was poor indeed. Copying masterpieces is not an easy task since one has to be faithful to the colors, the light and shadows, the enhancement of figures and the content overall. It takes real talent to copy and genuine interest in art styles and modes of painting to render a genuine copy. It also takes patience and perseverance and above all a keen eye for detail. One has to make sure that the colors she uses are those that approximate those used by the artist. Not just approximation, I would dare say, but faithful reproduction of colors. That takes a real knowledge of colors and their mixtures. One has to first study profoundly the painting *afin d'approfondir l'élément de créativité,* I would say. To see deeply and feel deeply the creativity of the artist in a particular painting. The realtionship between artist-maker and artist-copier must be extremely profound and just. One cannot simply try to imitate, but she has to attempt with the best of her artistic soul to endeavor transmitting the exactitude of a work of art. It's not dabbling and daubing at all. I knew when I approached a painting at the Louvre that I had to be on my best behavior as an artist myself, meaning I had the responsibility of not only duplicating a painting but creating precisely what I saw and even felt as an artist. I had to be perfect in my copying and my determination was to reach the ideal copy. How does one reach perfection, you might ask. Never. But, get to it as close as you can would be my answer. It's a goal. Not an impossible one but a high goal and it takes time, energy spent, and keen observation and above all a deliberate intent in doing one's best in applying one's creativity to the test of perfect imitation. I must have done very well since I was asked repeatedly to copy master after master for which I was paid a goodly sum of money. Finally, I was earning my keep and earning a reputation as a budding artist.

I loved Nicholas Poussin's work. Although classified as Baroque, his work goes beyond the Baroque, as far as I'm concerned. His paintings are characterized by clarity, logic, and order and favors line over color. He inspired artists even beyond the Baroque era in France. He stood apart from the popular tendency toward the decorative in French art of his time for which I admire him as an artist. Most of his paintings are mythological or biblical in nature, and I can understand the influence Rome had on the contents of his art. I especially liked one of his paintings that I copied, and that's the "Vision of Saint Paul." Ususally we see him thrown off his horse in Damascus, but this particular painting is mystical in its approach, since Paul is carried off by angels. What he sees, we do not know. At least, I don't. There are three angels, one of which is hidden except for some glimpses of his blue garb. The others we see quite plainly. One has a shadowy garb while the one to the left has a bright orange-yellow garb with bright golden folds. The angels and Saint Paul are all barefoot for whatever reason. I well understand that heavenly creatures do not wear shoes but the apostle Paul must have worn sandals. Saint Paul gazes heavenward since he is in the process of having a vision of some kind. The background is filled with shadowy thick clouds with a slight break in the center. Below, resting on a pillow, is a long sword most probably representative of the way he was going to die as a Roman citizen. Far away at a distance is a hill and village of some kind to remind us the earthbound side of Paul as a missionary to the Gentiles. The angels are anthropomorphic, and here we see the collaboration of human and the divine. What intrigued me and fascinated me was Saint Paul's bright red cloak right in the center of the painting. It truly catches one's eye. It probably has some kind of symbolic interest attached to it, such as red as the color of blood he was to shed or even for a simple touch of astonishing color to focus on. Otherwise, the painting would seem drab and unattractive. I do not mean that this touch is decorative because Poussin was not the artist of decoration. It is a highlight of Baroque rendering to a painting that pulses with clarity and meaningful attention given to a subject that resonates with biblical implications. I am not a religious person and I would not choose this type of subject for one of my paintings, but I do admire the vivacity and creative vigor that Poussin brings to this painting, especially the red cloak. I kept on staring at it all the while I was copying this masterpiece. There are so many other paintings of Nicholas Poussin in the Louvre and away in other museums, but I choose to describe this particular one for you as a sample of his enormous talent and productivity as an artist.

The next artist is Peter Paul Rubens, a great artist with enormous talent. I was so glad to be able to copy some of his works. He's a Flemish Baroque painter with a style that emphasizes movement, color and sensuality which is not my penchant. He ran a large studio in Antwerp and was a man with a Renaissance humanist education which I do not have and never aspired to it, although I admire those who have it. In his paintings, the female model is a full-figured highly sensualized being known now as Rubenesque. The male figures represent highly athletic and large mythical or biblical males. The concepts Rubens artistically represents illustrate the male as powerful, capable, forceful and compelling. I have seen several of these figures. However, I was asked to copy a particular work in the series of Marie de Medici, and I chose the sketch of Marie de Medici's "Arrival in Marseille", a very Baroque work in style and content blending some form of reality with mythology and symbolism. A busy work, I call it, with many characters. Marie de Medici is stepping out of a very ornate ship under an open half cupula-like or shell-like exit with ladies-in-waiting around her and a welcoming allegorical soldier bowing to her with open arms personifyng France, wearing a helmet and the royal blue mantle with the golden fleur-de-lis. Marie de Medici is disembarking and arrives in Marseille after having been married to Henry IV by proxy in Florence. She is dressed regally in fine flowing white satin while there are bare-breasted nymphs, or rather mermaids in the water, watching her arrival. Next to them stands an old man with a long white beard, and next to him a younger nude man holding a trident. Carved into the wooden prow of the ship is the figure of a woman. Above in the sky hovers what seems to me the figure of a man with flowing blue garb. I did not nor do I recognize the symbolism of all these figures in this what I call *oeuvre foisonnante,* busy work. It's a sketch but a marvelous one, one that taught me to do sketches all the more before attempting to do the actual painting. This sketch is very close to the actual finished product, I'm sure. I painstakingly copied this famous work and achieved success at it. It is said that Rubens turned something ordinary into something of unprecedented magnificence. However, as much as I admire Peter Paul Rubens, I would never execute such a painting myself. It's too crowded and filled with figures that are not realistic, but rather symbolic. Symbolism is not my cup of tea, as they say.

The next painter that I dealt with was Salvator Rosa, an Italian Baroque painter who was considered to be extravagant and unorthodox. A perpetual rebel. The painting that I copied is called "Saul and the Witch of Endor". It's a phantasmogoric painting to say the least. It deals with a biblical subject, that of Saul, king of the Israelites, bent down before the shade of the prophet Samuel who is covered with a white shroud on which the light of the fire shines with eerie whiteness. Saul has on armor with a cloak of bright orange-golden color. The folds are well painted here. The Bible recounts that Saul learns of his fate and that David will succeed him. The entire painting has a gloomy even macabre atmosphere with bony horse heads, bat-winged skeletons, and owls with glowing eyes in the background. Truly a scary work. It is said that Rosa was a romantic before Romanticism. I do not know if it's true but the painting certainly reveals that quality of romantic overtones and style. I like Rosa's craft and talent for painting unusual creative scenes, but I cannot say that I like his paintings overall, especially this one. However, I did what I was asked to do and got to admire the skill of the artist as a painter. I did learn from Rosa and applied myself that much more in my learning stage of creating art.

Now, I want to talk about Paulus Potter and his work as an artist. He died of tuberculosis at the age of 28, so young and so soon when his full capacity as an artist was in bloom. He was a Dutch painter of animals and landscapes, and that's why I greatly admire his skills as an artist and especially his choice of subject matter that I can so easily relate with. After all, I'm an *animalière,* am I not? I was asked to copy the Louvre's original painting of "Le Cheval Pie" the "Piebald Horse" recognized as one of his great paintings. I enjoyed doing the copy but I mostly enjoyed doing research on Paulus Potter and his other works and found a print of his "Young Bull" and "Four Bulls" as well as his "Two Pigs in a Sty." Now, not everyone would enjoy looking at a painting of two pigs, but I truly enjoyed this painting. It's so true-to-life and downright realistic that you could touch the two beasts and even smell them so real are they painted with every detail, every bit of porcine hair on both pigs, the fell hay, the slits in the wooden sty letting in some light, and above all, the faces and snouts of these animals. These animals are certainly not idealized; they are real. I admire the realistic touch of the artist and I learned so very much from him. I certainly transferred his keen sense of observation and his artistic rendition to my own discipline as an artist. You see, we artists learn from each other. Art is not spontaneous nor is it a talent that is completely free and clear of influences. I bow to the great artists who inspired me and gave me the incentive to progress deliberately, progressively and artistically in my quest to become an artist of worth and merit. What really counts is the self-worth that flows from an artist's paint and brushstrokes. First, there is the conception of the work, then the actualization of it while maintaining the flow of creative juices and actually becoming one with the emerging painting. Once I begin a painting, I feel that I become enthralled with the subject that I am painting and totally absorbed by the act of painting with colors once I have done sketch after sketch to assure myself that I'm on the right artistic path of creativity. I become one with the painting itself and I am mesmerized by it to the point that it haunts me even in my dreams. It may sound crazy to some but that's the way things are with me.

As for Karel Dujardin, I love his rendition of landscape scenes with animals such as "Cows and Sheep at a Stream", *"Bocage; Vaches, Anes et Moutons près d'un Ruisseau."* I enjoyed copying this one. It's such a peaceful and tranquil scene. The animals seem perfectly content just being there. He is yet another Dutch artist. The Netherlands truly furnished us with so many painters known around the world hailed for their mastery of the brush and color. This particular painting is one that features animals on the grass next to a stream and simply and quietly enjoying the sun. The cows reflect the harmony of the countryside and the peaceful existence of the love of the bovine by the natives. The other animals, the sheep facing us are ingeniously painted with the light of the sun shining on them and all around them so that they appear to be radiant with color that the artist has applied with mastery and diligent care.

In this painting there are two cows, one standing and the other one lying down. There are two sheep and one lamb while the ass in lying in the shade of the trees. We can barely see it. Dujardin has artistically handled the long tall tree with scintilating gold leaves that gives height to the painting. The sky is pure Boucher in essence with a rich blue color and puffy clouds. The setting serene and awe-inspiring, at least it is to me. I really like this painting and I'm glad I got to copy it at the Louvre. The painting gave me, as we say in French, *des frissons de beauté*, shivers of beauty, and I could not stop staring at it with goose bumps going up and down my arms. Crazy isn't it?

Finally, in my list of preferences at the Louvre as part of my copying job, there's Louis Léopold Robert, a Swiss painter. It is unfortunate that the artist committed suicide in front of his easel bitterly discouraged and painfully without hope of lasting success. However, he did give us some fine works worthy of our consideration. One that I copied at the Louvre is "Summer Reapers Arriving in the Pontine Marshes." It's a work dealing with gypsies. Robert also dealt with brigands, we are told. I suppose he liked the outcasts or those in the margin of society. It does not matter to me. What matters are his colors and the style of painting. I especially like, in this painting, the two black oxen pulling the wagon on which four people are either standing or some sitting. There's a young woman with a child in her arms. A man with a sword above his head dances to the side while another is playing some kind of bagpipe. There is merriment here. There are other people around, but the one I want to focus on is the black curly-haired man with an open white shirt leaning against the wagon. He stands daringly proud and bold between the heads of the two deep black oxen. He holds a long pole and stands there flaunting his masculine sensuality with his hips a bit skewed. His eyes are on the two young peasant girls, one holding a sheaf of wheat. There is movement, or at least anticipated movement in this romantic depiction of *gitans* arriving at the marshes. Several people and critics branded this painting as romantic. I don't know too much about the -isms applied to art and literature, since I do not care about artistic movements in history, but I do care about the mastery of colors and brushstrokes. I care about the application of colors and the melding of various shades of colors. I do care about the representations of animals, and all I see in this painting are the heads of oxen although well depicted on canvas by an artist who knew how to paint and use colors appropriately and with artistic talent. I know that I myself would not paint such a canvas, but I do respect the talent of Louis Léopold Robert. *Prière de me pardonner moi et mes observations sur mes artistes de préférence au Louvre,car je ne veux pas vous ennuyer avec cela*, please forgive my annoying you with these preferences of artists at the Louvre. All I wanted to do was show you my work at this sanctuary of art and my work in copying masterpieces even though I may not consider all of them *chef-d'oeuvres,* but that's my evaluation of these works. At the very least, it was a learning experience for me and I valued its worth in my career as an artist. It heightened my desire to fulfill the promise I had made to myself, work hard so as to realize your dream to paint essentially animals...which I did, wouldn't you say?

CHAPTER THREE

MICAS. The name Micas is terribly important for me. It's the family name of my good and sympathetic friends who saved me from becoming desperate and without resources. They gave me confidence in myself and my art. You see, after my mother's death, I felt so alone that I wanted to be left alone and die. Why? Because I had lost the only real support in my young life. Few people realized my situation then, not even my father. Not even my relatives. However, the Micases came to my help and never abandoned me. I became their friend and close enough to become a member of their family. I will never forget this. Not even now. Madame Micas and her daughter, Nathalie, became my very good friends. As for Nathalie, she was my very best of friends. I had so very few then. The whole family Micas encouraged me to stick to my plans in becoming a full-fledge artist. I told them that women artists were not very popular with the people and especially with the critics, but they encouraged me to pursue valiantly my dreams. That such dreams should not be surpressed but enlightened with the power of creativity. True talent is never hidden, they told me, it is never hidden under a bushel basket, but rather shared and expanded. That's why they encouraged me to have my very own studio. I owe them so much, the Micases.

I have to talk about them and especially Nathalie since they played such an important role in my life. As for Nathalie, she was gifted with a romantic imagination claiming to be of Iberian origin. That's why we surnamed her Ines dellas Sierras, the Great Agnes, after a story by Charles Nodier. She always wore gaudy clothes and mostly fond of the colors red and black, dramatic colors. Energetic and a woman of action, Nathalie was never afraid to act if the occasion warranted it. She always pretended to possess medical skills and often acted as vetinerary surgeon when the occasion arose in the menagerie. She early on conceived a taste for painting with a preference for cats. One painting of hers was of a cat playing with a ball of yarn. It was an awful daub, but not wanting to discourage her, I added a few touches to this wretched piece myself. I must also say that Nathalie was overly sentimental, could not take a joke and ever played the lady. She could not help herself, I know. *Elle berçait des rêves de grandeur,* she nursed feelings of grandeur. Why, I remember saying about her, "Sometimes I think Nathalie would have made a fine wife for one of the court jesters of the olden time." Of course, I did not really mean that, and I would not have said it to her face, but I sensed it deep inside me and could not resist voicing it in some fashion. I never liked people who played the dramatic game of self-elevation, as I used to say, the game of elevating oneself in public to be admired and treated like a highly respected lady of absolutely no genuine merit. It's hypocrisy. Of course, Nathalie was never hypocritical, just self-delusional, I think. I loved Nathalie and her mother for they were people of good will and excellent appeal. They would not ever hurt a fly and never trample on anyone. They were genuine friends, except friendship does not hide the flaws beneath it, especially mine. Yes, I know I have faults and I recognize them, but I do not intentionally exhibit them, and I try to reconcile my good side with my bad. Yes, we all have bad sides. The bad sides are the ones that hinder us in our pursuit of staying on the right road. But, I am not religious nor am I one who preaches to others. I just tried to do my best with people and did my very best with the talents God had given me. I tried to improve on them by exercising them the best I could with multiple experiences through hard work and observation. Observation with a keen eye, now there's the tool to make artistic talents grow. Nathalie knew this and told me ever so often that she wished she had that particular talent. I told her to be more vigilant and stop dreaming. She answered that was her talent and her nature and she could not stop dreaming about things. After all, she said, what would life be without dreams. I left her to her dreams.

Madame Micas died a few years before Nathalie and both of them were buried in the family vault at Père Lachaise cemetery in Paris. That's where I asked to be buried along with my faithful and beloved friend Anna Klumpke. I'll introduce her to you shortly. Yes, she will also appear as *une revenante* later on to talk about my work, but not before I tell you about my official permission to wear trousers in public. I'm the one who will tell you about it and no one else since no one else knows the real reason behind it. It was not because I wanted publicity or a manly look, not even the appearance of being stranger than every other woman my age. No, it was for the simple reason that I could work better and more easily

and more comfortably free from whatever hampered me from walking around and observing animals in the slaughterhouses where men were the only persons allowed there, or at least, the only ones who could be there without someone staring incessantly at them. I was going there to learn. That's all. Learn what? Well, learn about the structure, contours, and the many muscles and anatomical features of the animals I would see there without being scrutinized by a man who would think that this was not the place of a woman. I looked shockingly manly, me and my square jaw, bold features and short hair, certainly not refined as a lady would, so that it was easy enough for me to pass as just another being without too much fuss about sex and feminine demeanor. All I wanted to do was to to enhance my chances of becoming a well-informed artist as an *animalière,* as you call me. I never called myself that but I accepted the name since that's what I did, paint animals and I loved my craft as an artist, as long as people left me alone to enjoy the freedom of painting animals. I loved animals and they were good to me. They let me enter their world, a world of natural wonder and sacredness. Yes, sacredness since I've always believed that the animal world or kingdom as some say it, is a world that is blessed by the Great Creator who determined that this earth needed and deserved animals from the very beginning of creation. Think of it, what would the world be without animals? Senseless and without real and natural beauty. Sure, we would have the forests and the flowers and the birds and the bees and so forth and bees, and birds are animals. But, oh, the majesty of a horse, the fidelity of a dog and the valiant presence of a lion with a full mane. When I painted animals, I felt that I personnally entered a new world of living creatures where nature and humans came into a harmony established a long long time ago perhaps called the primieval times or whatever. Some people took the biblical words either literally or for granted when the Creator told the humans to take dominion over the animals and everything else in creation. But that was not a decree to take over everything without consideration for these creatures and do whatever they wanted to do even if it meant slaughtering, abusing, demeaning, hating, and even destroying them for their financial worth such as the trunks of elephants for ivory. No, we must realize that all of creation is a trust granted us and we must handle this trust with dignity and even compassion. Why do I care about a dog, a horse, a lion, a bird, or even the tiniest insect? Because I was entrusted with their care so that all of the animals in the world would live free and without danger of human violent interference. That's what I thought and will ever think, even if I am dead and speaking to you as a *revenante.*

Now, for the details of my special permission to be allowed to wear trousers in public. They called it *"Permission de Travestissement."* I got it at the *Préfecture de Police* dated May 12, 1857 and duly signed, stating that I was allowed to be dressed as a man, *de s'habiller en homme,* mind you, and *pour raison de santé,* yes, that's what it said, for health reason, and furthermore with restrictions against attending spectacles, balls or other public meeting places, *autres lieux de réunion ouverts au public.* As if I was going to expose myself publicly to all and everyone dressed in trousers. Besides, were trousers only the domain of men, I asked myself. I did not care as long as I would be left free at the slaughterhouses. I wasn't going to take the carriage and go to Paris balls. I was not going to show my so-called lack of intelligence, intelligence that only men had, as some people thought, and go romping around in trousers smoking a cigarette, although I loved smoking cigarettes...in private.

As far as slaughterhouses are concerned, I remember writing somewhere at some time this, "To perfect myself in the study of nature I spent whole days in the Roule slaughterhouse. One must be greatly devoted to art to stand the sight of such horrors, in the midst of the coarsest people." They wondered at seeing a young woman taking interest in their work and made themselves as disagreeable to me as they possibly could. *Lorsque notre but est juste,* when our aims are right, we always find the necessary help. Providence sent me a protector in the good Monsieur Émile, a butcher of great physical strength. He declared that whoever failed to be polite to me would have to reckon with him. I was thus enabled to work undisturbed.

Yes, good old Monsieur Émile, he was such a kind individual. I remember I had the figure of a young boy then and my hair was cut short so that I looked somewhat like most teenage boys. Besides, my father had already told me that I had the demeanor of a boy rather than a girl, and that if I did not change I would definitely not grow up to be a lady. As if I cared being a lady or not. All that mattered to me then was learning about animals from many perspectives. I was going to do things scientifically, especially in my art work and learn the anatomical science of animals. I really did not care about what they called demeanor, comportment and lady-like manners, not even what they called decorum. That was for other young girls who cared more for balls, parties and extravaganzas and above all young men. Such things were not priorities in my book.

Some people started comparing me with George Sand, but she had her own way of doing things and appearing in public. She was George Sand and that's all, a literary figure. People in literature have special privileges, I suppose, or they take them and call them their own without too much consideration of what people might say or think about them. I was not a George Sand and neither a *grisette*, a common working girl mind you. I was Rosa Bonheur, the woman artist who loved painting animals and was going to do whatever it took to become an artist of mastery who revered naturalism and painted the way she saw things and not necessarily felt things, although I could not separate my thoughts and my feelings about animals. What I observed and what I studied with as keen an eye as I could muster, I painted with interest and even, I might say, passion. Yes, passion, for the word connotes intense ardor for what one likes and does. One could say that *j'ai toujours eu la passion des animaux et de les peindre avec ardeur, une ardeur qui sort de mes seins et même de mes entrailles de femme indépendente...* I always had the passion for animals and painting them with ardor, the ardor that juts from my bosom and my guts as an independent woman. I'm being a bit melodramatic here, I think. I did go to a slaughterhouse, more than once, to become an artist of worth and intense desire to render what is real in nature, the reality of life and living. I believe I did and I did it with my art and did it very well, I'll have you know. Enough of myself and my history. Speaking of George Sand and literature, I must admit that I did not read many literary works. I read some but not as much as others around me did. However, my very favorite book was "Don Quixote, the Man from La Mancha." I found that the story by Cervantes amazingly interesting. I loved Don Quixote and his mad wanderings as a knight-errant, although he wasn't as mad as some people may think. Even the author must have known that because he shows us quite often the hidden intelligence of his hero. I know some people think that tilting with windmills is rather stupid on his part but that's what Romanticism does to many people. I should say the Romanticism of the Middle Ages and the many stories about knights and demoiselles in castles reading about the adventures of knighthood in full bloom. That's what happens when one is given to too much reading and doesn't realize that life is not in books but in the reality and practice of things. Observation and experience, that's what makes life a true adventure. That's what I wanted to bring to my art and I did my very best to attain it.

Be it as it may, what I want you to know about me is my artwork, my paintings and the best person to tell you all about it is my very best friend whom I met the same year that Nathalie Micas died. She was an American and had her own talent as an artist. But, I will let her tell you about herself and then about my paintings. You will like her even as a *revenante* . My bones and her ashes are in the same vault at Père Lachaise. So are the Micases bones. *Adieu, chers lecteurs et lectrices.* Perhaps, I will see you later.

CHAPTER FOUR

I am Anna Klumpke, Anna Klumpke, Klumpke, Klumpke. What a heavy-sounding name like a clump of something. I was a clump alright, a lame woman who had a hard time walking straight due to an accident as a child, and worst of all, I had an extraordinary large nose for a woman. Rosa Bonheur used to tell me that most of the time. Not to insult me but to make a comment about what she considered evidently long, like Cyrano de Bergerac's grotesque nose. She loved that play. She may tell you that she did not read much, but she did. Her reading list consisted of "Don Quixote" by Cervantes, Rostand's "Cyrano de Bergerac," James Fenimore Cooper, Walter Scott, of course LaFontaine and all his amazing tales of animals, Buffon, Eugène Sue, George Sand and Le Brun. She also read animal anatomy books to enlighten herself about the make-up of animals.

Rosa Bonheur and I were very close friends for some ten years until her death in 1899. I hope you will trust my statements as a user of words outlining and describing the many paintings that Rosa Bonheur created in her lifetime. Even as a *revenante* I can communicate with you in all truthfulness and sincerity. Like Rosa Bonheur I was granted the special gift of telling you my experiences as the live-in companion of this unique artist that was Rosa Bonheur. Yes, I lived at the Chateau de By and shared so many enjoyable moments with the artist who was known as an *animalière remarquable* . She was a remarkable woman, a woman who became a pioneeer in animal painting for her time. Others had done animal painting, but there was no one like her. Hers was a monster talent, to say the least. Not that I like using the term monster, but that's what it means, beyond the ordinary and beyond the expectations of those who only await ordinariness and banality of talent. I could go on and on about Rosa Bonheur, but I'm not here to celebrate wildly the woman. I'm here to share my experiences, knowledge, and observations about her art. And, that's what I will do to the best of my ability.

First of all, I need to say a little bit about myself so that you may get a glimpse of the woman who lived with Rosa Bonheur for so many years, and got to know her more and perhaps better than herself.

I was born in San Francisco. I was an American who had a very ambitious mother who was determined to bring her five daughters to Paris. This was to compensate, she insisted, for a provincial early childhood in San Francisco. I attended the Académie Julien in Paris and did very well in my studies. I even won an honorable mention in the Salon of 1885. Yes, I learned how to draw and paint, and I was very good at it. My biggest wish then was to meet Rosa Bonheur, my model and inspiration. How I wished this as much as a young girl wishes for the moon and the stars. My luck had it that my wish was indeed in the stars because I did get to meet Rosa Bonheur in person in 1889 when I accompanied John Arbuckle, a prosperous coffee merchant. I was brought to the Chateau de By as a translator. I was thirty-three years old then and had dreamed of meeting Rosa Bonheur for years, but it had never come to fruition until then. Mister Arbuckle came to meet Rosa Bonheur at her Chateau de By to take a look at the three wild mustangs he had sent her from his ranch in Wyoming, a few years earlier. I was ecstatic, to say the least. I did have a bit of a difficulty with horse terms, as I called them, but Rosa Bonheur helped me along, and was quite sympathetic to my situation as translator to an American who could hardly speak a word of French. But, talk, did he talk, while I had a hard time following his utterances. I could see the smile on Rosa Bonheur's face now and then. I simply felt nervous and quite mortified by the awesome task of absorbing English words, American English words, that were almost immediately transformed or phonetically transcribed into French words coming out of my mouth. There I was honing the rough cultural edges of an American rancher and merchant and presenting the best I could a man of horse knowledge and abilities. He was an intelligent man, Mister Arbuckle, but a man of very little cultural knowledge and sensitivity, a kind of nouveau-riche whose money opened doors for him. However, it worked and worked out well overall. Rosa Bonheur was delighted and both of us right there and then formed a budding friendship that lasted for years to come. That's how I met Rosa Bonheur, the astonishing painter of animals. I was to paint her portrait later on, but that's much later in our relationship as master and student of art. I never stopped learning from her and she was ever sensitive to my strengths and my failings, and, of course, my big nose. She enjoyed my playing the piano since it reminded her of her mother, Sophie, and her musical talent. As much as I was attached to my mother, Rosa Bonheur was enormously fond of her mother, Sophie, for she took every occasion she could to talk about her, and how she thought she was a saint. The only thing she regretted about her was that she had died a pauper's death and her bones were lost in some unknown graveyard somewhere. How I wished I could have consoled her and told her where those bones were, but it could not be done, not by me nor by anyone else. It was part of the destiny of a poor suffering woman who had very little and tried desperately to hold on to whatever she could get a hold of. I only wished then that I could have known Sophie and paint her portrait. That would have been a lasting legacy to leave to a disheartened daughter. Wishes do not always materialize, I know. They often vanish and we are left with their memory.

Before I go on with Rosa Bonheur's works, I feel I must talk about one word with its meaning that exemplified Rosa Bonheur's values and trust in people and animals that were part and parcel of her entire life, and that is RELATIONSHIP. Relationship was a most important word in Rosa Bonheur's vocabulary. She often talked about it with me and I was justifiably impressed by her conviction dealing with relationships in her lifetime as a person and as an artist. First of all, there was the relationship with her dear mother, Sophie, whom she loved and adored. Her entire life was permeated with this loving and enduring relationship between mother and daughter. Pedagogically, Sophie was an ideal mother for she taught her daughter how to read and write using illustrations of animals to stimulate Rosa's imagination and learning skills. Even beyond the grave, Sophie still communicates with her daughter and protects her from any harm or unwise decision, says Rosa Bonheur. As for the father, Raimond, it was a strained and wayward relationship with Rosa since his affection for her was unexpressed and very limited. He was not a loving person and he had a very hard time establishing relationships that did not follow the dictates of his philosophy as a Saint-Simonian. He did teach his daughter how to draw and paint, but it was only a way to force her into an independent way of living. Rosa Bonheur transferred her love and caring after her mother's death to her close friend Nathalie Micas and her mother, Henriette. She needed to express her love and attachment to them since she had no one else to turn to. Theirs was a very close and endearing relationship that lasted until their death. As you shall see, Nathalie was an important factor in Rosa Bonheur's life and work. Then, I came along and filled the empty spot in Rosa Bonheur's life and soul. I was very close to her and I loved her dearly. She reciprocated this love and our relationship flourished. She was my model, my teacher and my loyal companion for ten years at Chateau de By.

As for the agent Gambart, theirs was not a relationship of love and attachment but a relationship based on business transactions and money. He did, however, open several doors for her but it seemed that he did so to favor their relationship out of personal interest. He did not like me and I did not like him. One person that struct a warm and even intimate relationship with Rosa Bonheur was the Empress Eugénie. By her sense of admirable dignity and her warm and endearing personality, the Empress sollicited from Rosa Bonheur her admiration and friendship. Theirs was a realtionship based on mutual admiration and trust. Rosa Bonheur also loved her younger brother, Isidore, and they shared a sympathetic chord with one another. The relationship between little brother and big sister was fundamentally natural and enduring. Rosa Bonheur never faltered in her relationship with Isidore. Finally, there was the express relationship with the animals on which Rosa Bonheur lavished her love and devotion. She had a very close relationship with all animals especially the horses that she admired for their strength and endurance and, of course, for her dear lioness, Fathma. Rosa Bonheur, the *animalière* was a gifted person and artist who developed and nurtured, throughout the years, a deep relationhsip with all animals that she encountred and painted. One might say without restraint that Rosa Bonheur's realtionship with people and animals was deep and everlasting insofar as her capability to endure and flourish was given to her. She never backed off from a realtionship that was dear and sincere to her heart and soul both as a person and as an artist.

Rosa Bonheur was convinced that her relationships had to be frank and honest for she would not waste her time and energy on any relationship that was flagging and dishonest, she once told me.

Well, now, where do I start with Rosa Bonheur's work as an artist? An accomplished artist who astounded the nation and even the world with her enormous talent as an *animalière*. Her accomplishment did not come easy to her. She had to work very hard at it and sometimes she had to struggle to find the right subjects and learn about each and everyone of them, animals of every kind. She drew sketches in order to make sure that what she was going to put on canvas was realistically, scientifically, and artistically true according to nature, but especially true according to her high standards of creativity and keen observation. My friend, Rosa Bonheur, was a perfectionist and sought to make her art the pivotal point of her life. She used to tell me that perfection did not exist but that she could, at the very least, come close to it, and she did. As far as I was concerned, she did just that.

I suppose the first place to start would be with her first painting of animals that was publicly recognized and admired, "Rabbits Nibbling Carrots." I did not grow up loving and handling animals even as pets, but I developed a liking for some animals while living at Chateau de By. Rosa Bonheur's love for animals was contagious in a way. Seeing her devotion to animals, all animals, made me see and appreciate how a human being could develop a certain bond with them. I did not paint them, but I had a certain fondness of the love imparted on them. "Rabbits Nibbling Carrots" is a work that reflects the sensitive and remarkable skill of the artist at work, and entirely devoted to the naturalness of the animals and their surroundings. That's what we have here. It was reported that people looking at this painting wanted to touch the two animals, so realistically painted were they. We see here two rabbits, one nibbling a carrot, a bright orange one, while the other is gazing rather furtively into space. We can only see one eye of each of the rabbits, and they're very well defined. The long ears of both of them are straight up as if anticipating the suspicious sounds that would surprise them. They are both fat and furry with short fur resembling velvety coats of brownish hair. One would even dare touch both animals so realistic have they been put on canvas with paint. One would even try to adopt them as pets since they are so inviting as warm and cuddly animals. Certainly, one would not destine them for the cooking pot. The two pieces of carrots as well as the highlighted white parsnip draw one's attention since they are at the very forefront. This is a simple painting, and by this, I mean a painting revealing the natural quality of the animals and the scene, as a whole, that the artist attempted to paint. Rosa Bonheur was nineteen when she did this, and it reveals her talent for painting animals as well as her capabilities to arouse feelings for artistic creation in the minds and hearts of the onlookers. I was told that this painting, as well as another one were hung without comments at the 1841 annual Paris Salon, and that her father was extremely proud of her.

Of course, Rosa Bonheur did many paintings and was ever active in her craft as an artist . She loved aninals and therefore used many of them as the subjects of her paintings such as, "Animals Grazing, Evening Effect"*[Animaux dans un pâturage---effet du so*ir]; "Sheep in a Meadow" *[Moutons dans une prairie]; "Studies of Pureblood Stallions"[Études de chevaux étalons pur sang]* and "Grazing Sheep" *[Moutons au pâturage]*. All four of these were shown at the Salon. My very favorite was "Evening Effect" because I loved the light and darkness effect of the colors that she used. However, the one painting that struck a chord with me and with so many admirers was "Ploughing in the Nivernais"[*Le Labourage nivernais*]. It's a magnificent piece full of vitality and precision of craft. It's a humble subject as such, but the painting reflects the industriousness and strength of character of the *laboureurs.* When I told Rosa Bonheur of my boundless admiration for this painting, truly a masterpiece, she was indeed a bit stunned by my remarks, especially when I dared to show my American presumption of asking her to copy the painting. As soon as I began to understand the gift of her marvelous talent of interpreting nature with such masterful energy, I realized what a difficult task it had been to paint such a masterpiece, and what a horrendous task it was for me even to copy it. But, I did it and it was a fine copy. I was even able to sell it.

As for the painting itself, the farm labor of the two farmers is often qualified as *sombrage* due to the first labor in early autumn when the soil is opened up and the plough sinks into the ground after a long waiting period of summer. The oxen at the plough are of the race of the Morvan, known for their strength and ability to pull and plough. There was a realist interest in rural society at that time and Rosa Bonheur captured that interest with deep and sincere strokes of her valiant effort to imitate nature and peasant labor, just as George Sand had done in her popular novel "The Devil's Land" in which she describes the nobility of animals alongside the peasants. Rosa Bonheur told me that she had enjoyed reading this novel and was highly impressed by it.

In this particular painting, we see two teams of oxen pulling wooden ploughs and guided by two peasant farmers. Looking at the entire work, one cannot but notice the beautiful and vast expanse of the sky treated with softened light and clarity often seen in Dutch paintings which Rosa Bonheur had studied and copied in the Louvre, particularly the works of Paulus Potter that she so admired as an accomplished artist.

Two teams move forward slightly uphill. The strong muscles, the shaggy texture of fur and the determined expression on their faces, as well as their slow but arduous steps in the upturned soil, are all there to notice and appreciate. At least, I did. There are no yokes. The animals are only led by voice commands. The land being ploughed is depicted with such accuracy that one can almost smell the rich moist soil being turned in the early autumn afternoon. What an artistic accomplishment on Rosa Bonheur, the artist's part we see here. I was at first overwhelmed, then inspired enough to put my hand to the brushes, the colors, the canvas that awaited me to apply the first brushstrokes after I had sketched the outlines that I desired. I was going to follow in the magical footsteps of Rosa Bonheur, I told myself, magical because it was just that for me, perhaps even mystical in some fashion. I was all nervous and excited about this project of mine, one that Rosa Bonheur herself approved of and even delighted in, as she told me later. One can only feel the ardor and passion of painting when one is completely immersed in it, and the labor of artistic love and creativity is one that can hardly be expressed into words. Perhaps literary figures can, but I cannot. Rosa Bonheur had a splendid vocabulary and often wrote long letters to friends and acquaintances, but her mastery of expression was in her art. At least, that's what I think. People who admired her paintings as well as the critics who wrote about them and her ability to express her passion for painting so well, they all think that way. They still do after so many years.

Now, I want to talk about Rosa Bonheur herself as a woman. She is the one who asked me to write her memoirs of her life story as an artist .

She did not trust anybody else, she told me. I told her that not only was I going to cover her artistic life but her personal life as much as she trusted me to do so, and she agreed. I did not want to pry into her very personal life, but she asked me to be frank and sincere about it and to delve, if I wanted to, into her personal life as a woman and an artist. She told me that she would guide me all the way as long as I remained faithful to my task as biographer and personal confidant. She trusted me and I trusted her words. She would never lie to me, that I knew. Trust in a person is sacred. It was so for Rosa Bonheur as it was for me. That was part of our relationship, Rosa Bonheur and I, a relationship that would last as long as we lived together. What good is it to cover the truth so as to remain superficially glossy and nice and appealing to those who love and are loved. What good are glossed over lies?

Rosa Bonheur was a good person and an honest person. She could not tolerate lies and cover-ups. Many people tried to read malice and lies into her lifestyle as a celibate woman, a woman of strong mind and will, who smoked cigarettes and wore trousers. Furthermore, she had a sincere and deep devotion to some particular women such as Nathalie Micas and, of course, myself. She would tell you herself that these relationships were not couched in sex nor what is called today as lesbianism. Rosa Bonheur's love for certain women was chaste and pure and not tainted with strong desires to sleep with them. Some people wondered about her living with me at the Chateau de By and what transpired there. Well, what transpired at the Chateau was deep affection on the part of both parties, Rosa Bonheur and myself, mutual admiration in art and culture and for Rosa, the great love of animals that she so cherished. I shared her love for animals but not as deeply and strong as she did. We both did paintings in our way of applying colors on canvas as well as sketching. Rosa Bonheur loved sketches and she did hundreds of them if not thousands. She really wanted to get things right about her painting when she was ready to apply paint to a canvas. You could say that she was an idealist when it came to the art of painting. Painting was truly an art and not just a craft for her. She was so meticulous about it. She was a true *animalière* and spent long hours studying animals, animals that she grew to love and even cherish like her pet lioness, Fathma. How she loved that animal probably more than she loved people. Her love of animals inspired her to paint with passion, a strong feeling and expression that grew out of her love of animals. One example of course is her great love of horses, as you can see in the "Horse Fair", a monstrous painting. I call it monstruous since it is bigger than life and reality, although she was a true realist. But, that painting elicits strong feelings about art and horses. That's why people were drawn to it, people and critics too. It was and is magnificent, and I might add grandiose in my opinion. It's bigger than life and it raises one's spirit to a level of awe and wonderment. The movement, the powerful strength of the horses, the texture of the color and light with shadows and the skill of the painter in transfering on canvas what she herself saw and conceived is unimaginable in my way of seeings things. She was truly an artist *hors pair,* out of the mold, for she became a model of perfection in painting animals and landscapes. I admired her to a point of slavish admiration, you might say. That is why I so wanted to meet her and it was a dream fulfilled whern she asked me to live with her and share her atelier that she herself had created at Chateau de By. Rosa Bonheur was truly a creative woman filled with hopes and ideas that would transcend anyone's hopes and ideas. She lived in a world of creativity and realism all to herself. She tried to impart that sense to me, but I could not attain it to the level she wished me to grasp. And so, I tried to imitate her and learned a lot from her. She was my muse, my angel of inspiration and my beloved consort, woman to woman, who thrive on a realtionship that is built on respect, admiration and sincere love for one another. Now if you want to see sexual and carnal love and attachment into this, well that's your bias and I leave that to all of you out there who do not see clearly the chaste and devoted love of two women living as companions and fellow artists. That's all I have to say about that, and that's all Rosa Bonheur would ever say about that too. We do not need to explain ourselves nor excuse ourselves for our lifestyle. We know the truth behind our living together and we have no qualms about it since we led chaste lives and creative lives. All of our energies were directed toward our art and we thrived on it. My art and my output were not as great as Rosa Bonheur's but they weren't bad, if I say so myself. Even she admired what I did especially the portraits I did of her. I think they were simply magnificent, if you do not mind my bragging. You see, Rosa Bonheur channeled her artsitic energies into me and my talent for painting by giving me her insights into things, and by offering me her way of capturing reality and frankness that she so treasured. I do not know if I absorbed it well but I know that I did make it part of me and my way of seeing things. Rosa Bonheur was a splendid teacher for she taught by her very own experiences and commitment to perfection in art. And she worked hard at it, very hard indeed. Nothing comes easy in art, she would say, nothing. Not if you want to produce true art, the art of rendering in a true creative way what you see and what you experience. From palette to brush to canvas there's a long and even perilous struggle that very few realize except the dedicated artist, she used to say. I have to admit that I felt the same way, and I got to admire her for her strong-willed determination to reach an ideal in her art, the art that she, Rosa Bonheur, was so passionate about. And, she succeeded. I firmly believe that. Of course, I may be a bit prejudiced, but so many people view her and her paintings that way.

I must say at this point that her attachment to women, particular women, stems from the loss of a woman that was so terribly dear to her, her mother, Sophie. She lost her when she was very young and saw in that loss a person who had nourished her and loved her and encouraged her to be who she was potentially going to become in life. She truly loved her mother. Besides, she realized that the woman who was Sophie, her mother, lived a life of hardships, struggles and penury. However, she never complained and never sought to blame her husband, Raimond, who left her and the children to fend for themselves without too much money for their necessities. Raimond, the father, was a good man but an idealist and a Saint-Simonian who cared more for the cause of socialism than his family. The mother must have felt abandoned and alone in her misery but she was a good mother, a saintly woman, Rosa Bonheur told me. Rosa revered her mother to a point that she felt a terrible loss when her mother died. I suppose Rosa Bonheur placed her dear mother on a pedestal and felt pain and delusion when she discovered that her poor mother was buried with the poorest of the poor, unidentified and thrown into a pit with lime as most destitute and abandoned persons are. They lose their personhood, Rosa Bonheur said, and they are soon forgotten. However, Rosa never forgot her mother and kept her souvenir constantly in her heart and in her ardent mind. It was her way of salvaging the memory of one who had disappeared from her life when she needed a mother and a constant companion, the woman-mother-friend she craved for and needed.

Rosa Bonheur's international fame came to assuage the hurt she suffered for such a very long time, a hurt that would never go away, for her fame redounded on her mother, Sophie, who had taught her to read and register letters of the alphabet with drawings of animals. The loss of such a dear woman in Rosa's life became the instigation of the unique kind of love for other women with whom she surrounded herself and her grief for the rest of her life as an artist, an *animalière accomplie.* For you see, there is a very fine line between a mother's love and the love of a child for her mother, and the love of animals. All three of them are natural. Rosa Bonheur could not and would not separate them. She could not envision a world without animals nor could see a world deprived of motherly love. Rosa Bonheur did not always express her love for other women like Nathalie and myself in a way that was tangible and obvious but it was real. It was there. However, her love of animals was made real and clear in her ability to paint them with a realism that was filled with love and admiration. It took a lot of love and admiration of animals especially horses such as the Percherons to ask for official permission to wear trousers in public so she could go to the slaughterhouse and explore the reality of animals being sold and probably butchered, and others brought to the horse fair for selection and purchase. That love and admiration got translated into the realism she so wanted in her paintings. Even the slightest hair, the finest fur, the tiniest mark and the finest of sparkle in the eye were captured with precision and artistry by Rosa Bonheur when she painted animals. And, only after she had drawn and sketched her composition for days and even months at times. If I remember, she did one hundred plus sketches for her "Horse Fair." That's a lot of artistic devotion coupled with a very strong taste of perfection, natural perfection for if you want perfection, look for it in nature. Nature itself is the reflection of the perfection of the Creator, she once told me. Although she was not a religious person, Rosa Bonheur believed in God and she quite often prayed to him for guidance and mercy. I know. I was there. She believed in the other life, eternal life for she wanted, she knew, that one day she would be reunited with her mother in the afterlife. She also wanted to be reunited with Nathalie and so she wanted to be buried in the same vault at Père Lachaise in Paris awaiting final reunion with the ones she so dearly loved. Why? She made sure that I would be buried there in the Micas' vault. She made me swear it would be so. So where do you think my ashes were buried? At Père Lachaise, of course, in the Micases vault.

I need to talk to you about some more of Rosa Bonheur's paintings, but now I have to let the Empress Eugénie talk. She asked to say a few words about Rosa Bonheur and her internationally known works of art. Although she was not an *animalière* herself, she greatly admired the realism that Rosa Bonheur brought to her art. That and her love for animals. If you remember, the Empress visited Rosa Bonheur at Chateau de By more than once. She so admired that woman artist that she personally went to her atelier to bring her the Legion of Honor medal and pay respect to a woman she both admired and esteemed.

"*Laissez-moi parler à mon tour, Madame Klumpke. Je ne veux pas vous chasser, mais on m'a donné un peu de temps pour faire l'éloge de Rosa Bonheur. Oh, excusez-moi, il me faut parler en anglais afin que les lecteurs et lectrices puissent me comprendre...*Let me speak in turn. I do not want to chase you away but I have been given very little time to praise Rosa Bonheur and her work. Oh, excuse me, I have to talk in English,don't I, for the readers to be able to understand me." Here it is in my limited English. I knew enough English to hold a conversation at court and elsewhere, I'll have you know. Well, I was wife and consort to Emperor Napoleon III for twenty years. I don't need to tell you that for you must already know it. *Je ne sais pas,* excuse me please, but I do not know if I can tell you everything about our famous woman artist, Rosa Bonheur, but I will do my best to tell you what I got to know about her and her great work as an artist *de qualité.* Of course, I cannot and will not tell you volumes and volumes about Rosa Bonheur for I am not able to do just that. I have my limitations and I know my strengths and weaknesses. Being of royal birth and of imperial rank, discretion has to be my word of honor and my tenure of sacred pride as a woman of high esteem and faithfulness to my God and my Emperor. Rank has not only its privileges but also its responsibilities. Royal birth and imperial rank never did strike me as an absolute, although I recognized their worth. I was never crowned empress and consort to the Emperor Napoleon III, but a crown was fashioned specifically for me, a consort crown, for the great *Exposition Universelle* of 1855 and it was sold by the Third Republic. It is now in the Louvre for all to see. *Sic transit* *gloria mundi* as it is said, glory, whatever glory, disappears with time, or at least it fades away.

I was born in Granada, Spain of Spanish royalty and got to know my expected place in the world, thanks to my mother who was ever vigilant about it. We escaped the cholera outbreak and went to Paris where I began my formal education at the fashionable and traditionalist *Couvent du Sacré-Coeur.* Then followed the *Gymnase Normal* where I developed my athletic skills. Then came a boarding school for girls in Bristol, England to learn English. You see, I know English from my early years. My sister and I returned to Paris where we were placed under the tutelage of two English governesses, a Miss Cole and a Miss Flowers. After my father's death, we returned to Spain and thanks to my mother's role as a lavish society hostess, I was introduced to Queen Isabel II and her Prime Minister, and from then on my life was changed. Eventually I met Prince Louis Napoleon after he had become president of the Second Republic. He fell in love with me and later we got married. Of course, the Imperial family, the Council of Ministers, and the coteries of the palace, regarded this union as a biting and unwanted humiliation, but I did not care. Not a bit. I was to become the consort to the Emperor and the mother of *cher Napoléon Eugène Louis Jean Joseph Bonaparte, mon fils, le Prince Impérial.* Unfortunately, I discovered that my husband began to stray just like in the olden days of his youth and resumed his *petites distractions*, his infidelities, But I did not let it get to me. I was a strong woman, a woman of determination and zeal for the Imperial cause, I told myself. I did not care too much for sex anyway.

I traveled to Egypt to open the Suez Canal and officially represent *mon époux impérial.* I strongly advocated equality for women and tried unsuccessfully to convince *l'Académie Française* to elect the famous writer George Sand as its first female member. I worked very hard for my causes and for my faith. The great and terrible disappointment in my life and that of my husband was the Franco-Prussian War that was the cause of the overthrow of the Second Empire and our exile in England.

"*Avez-vous fini, Madame l'Impératrice? Retournons à nos moutons, s'il-vous-plaît. Après tout, il faut en finir avec les détails de votre vie, aussi importants qu'il ne le soient.* Let's put a stop to your many details of your life. After all, we need to get back to Rosa Bonheur."

"Soyez plus indulgente, Madame Klumpke, un peu plus gallante envers moi, après tout, je le mérite bien." Be more indulgent and a bit more gallant with me for I do merit that.

"Pas au ciel, chère dame, pas au ciel." Not in heaven, dear lady. *"Mais nous ne sommes pas au ciel encore. Nous sommes dans les sphères de l'imagination, je crois."* We are not in heaven yet. We are in the spheres of the imagination, I believe.

Well, after my husband's death and my dear, dear son's death six years later which came as a terrible shock to me, I continued to be involved with causes close to my heart, especially dertermined to seek equality of rights for all women. That's when I decided to visit Rosa Bonheur on a whim while taking a drive in the Fontainebleau area. I dropped in at the atelier at the Chateau de By with my ladies in waiting, officers, and uniformed court dignitaries following close behind. I could see that the artist was quite surprised at seeing me there with my retinue. I gave her my hand and she kissed it. I looked into her eyes and I could see awe and pleasure there. Rosa Bonheur showed me her several sketches and some of her paintings there in the altelier. I told her that I especially liked *Les Cerfs sur les Longs Rochers*, Deer at Long Rocks. Before leaving after an hour's visit, I invited her for lunch at Fontainebleau. She later received the invitation and responded with pleasurable delight and came for lunch dressed in her best feminine clothes. That was before my husband, the Emperor, died. Prior to going into the dining area, my husband, the Emperor, gave her his arm and led her what I call refined nourishment. I could see that she truly liked it as well as the conversation with the Emperor. I then took her out for a boat ride and there on the shore she met my son the Imperial Prince who later in the week went to visit her to take a look at her menagerie. I was told that she had hurried to change clothes but that my son had said afterwards he had wished she had not changed clothes, for he preferred seeing her in smock and trousers. That made me smile.

One year later, I paid Rosa Bonheur another visit and this time it was for a particular purpose, a regal purpose. I told her "Mademoiselle, I'm bringing you a jewel from the Emperor. His Majesty has given me permission to inform you that you're being made a knight in the Imperial Order of the Legion of Honor." I remember my exact words just as I said them to her. She was standing in front of me wide-eyed and impressed by the formal presentation that was to take place. That's when I pinned on her bodice the red ribbon with the gold cross . She was from then on a *Chevalier dans l'Ordre de la Légion d'Honneur,* a distinct honor that she cherished for the rest of her life, I was told. I was and still am very proud to be the godmother of the first woman artist to receive this high honor. I wanted to devote my last act as regent to showing that, as far as I was concerned, genius had no sex.

My comment, as Anna Klumpke, is that the Empress Eugénie was a fine lady, well-educated, a refined woman of grace and style, who had a sovereign grace about her that made her the fashion queen of Parisian society, people said. Everyone who was anyone in Parisian society knew very well that her clothes fashioned by the English designer of Haute-Couture, Charles Frederick Worth, was of prominent elegance and much sought after by the elite. All I know is that her hats tilted to one side, her ostrich feathers and her demeanor in general attested to the fact that she was indeed an Empress worth of dignity and reverence. Precisely what Rosa Bonheur gave the Empress, *un regard digne d'une artiste-génie et un accueil de révérence,* a dignified gaze and a reverent welcome. That's all I have to say.

CHAPTER FIVE

*A*ttendez *un moment vous autres, je veux mettre mon mot là-dedans. Je m'appelle Charlotte Clairdomaine, et je veux parler à mon tour. Je veux vous révéler certaines choses cachées à propos de Rosa Bonheur.* "Say it in English." *Moi, Mademoiselle Klumpke, je ne parle pas anglais. Je suis de la basse classe, pas comme vous autres. Surtout pas l'Impératrice, ça c'est de la classe, l'Impératrice Eugénie. Si les gens veulent savoir ce que je dis, bien l'auteur peut aussi bien traduire pour moi. Il le peut car c'est lui qui conduit l'affaire dans ce roman.* [Wait a moment there, I want to put in my two cents in this chatter. My name is Charlotte Clairdomaine, and I want to speak since my time has come to reveal certain things about Rosa Bonheur that nobody knows.]

J'ai connu Rosalie Bonheur, Rosalie est son vrai nom, lorsque je n'avais que treize ans. Elle en avait seize. Je la trouvais bien avancée pour son âge. Je veux dire, bien déniaisée. Je l'ai connue à Paris après que sa mère Sophie est morte. Pauvre petite mère, pauvre elle, malade et si pauvre, malade d'ennui et malade de n'avoir personne à qui se fier. [I got to know Rosa Bonheur, Rosalie was her real name when I was but thirteen years old. She was sixteen. I found her to be ahead of her age. I mean mature. I knew her in Paris after her mother died. Poor Sophie Bonheur, poor her, sick and so poor, sick of being lonely and having no one to rely on.] *Rosa s'ennuyait elle aussi malgré ses croquis, ses dessins et son attachement aux animaux. Elle aimait tant les animaux celle-là. On disait d'elle qu'elle grandirait avec la tête et la queue d'un animal tellement elle aimait les animaux. Elle s'aurait vautrée même dans la soue de cochons tellement elle se mettait au niveau des bêtes, sauvages et apprivoisés.* [Rosa felt lonely too in spite of her sketches, her drawings and her attachment to animals. She loved animals that one. It was said of her that she would grow up with the head and tail of an animal, so much did she love them. She would have wallowed in a pig's stye so much did she place herself at the level of wild and tame beasts.] *Oui, je l'ai bien connue, Rosa Bonheur. Je n'étais pas amie avec elle mais je la connaissais assez bien car elle fréquentait mes amis, surtout un jeune homme qui s'appelait Jean Leiderer, un jeune homme dont la famille était immigrée de l'Allemagne. Son père était sculpteur sur bois alors que sa mère jouait de la flute dans un petit orchestre assez réputé pour ses interprétations musicales.* [Yes, I got to know Rosa Bonheur quite well. I wasn't a friend of hers but I knew her well since she frequented my friends and especially a young man by the name of Jean Leiderer whose family had emigrated from Germany. His father was a wood sculptor and his mother played the flute in a small orchestra that enjoyed a good reputation for its musical interpretations.] *Rosa Bonheur s'est mise à fréquenter le jeune homme parce qu'il lui faisait de la façon et lui parlait des arts. Lui aussi, comme sa mère, il aimait la musique et en plus, il aimait sculpter le bois. Il faisait des petites sculptures d'animaux . Elle en raffolait. Les deux se sont mis à se fréquenter comme amis, et plus tard comme amis intimes. Je ne veux pas dire comme amants mais assez proches que les gens se sont mis à dire d'eux que c'était bien un signe de fiançailles prometteur*[Rosa Bonheur started to go out with the young man because he paid attention to her and talked to her about fine arts. He, like his mother, loved music as well as he loved sculpting wood . She went wild over it. Both of them started going out like friends and later only became very close to one another. I don't mean to say like lovers but close enough that people started saying that this was a sign of impending bethrotal.] *Mon frère, Daniel, était ami avec Jean et celui-ci lui racontait tout même ses petits péchés et ses petites délices d'amour avec Rosa Bonheur. Pas que celle-ci était remplie d'affection pour le jeune homme, mais elle le gardait proche d'elle dans son coeur, avait-elle raconté à son amie, Pauline Boulanger, et Pauline était amie de ma soeur, Rachel, qui aimait bavarder avec presque tout le monde, moi incluse, car j'étais sa petite soeur.* [My brother, Daniel, was friends with Jean and Jean used to tell him everything including his little pecadillos. Not that Rosa was filled with affection for the young man, but she did keep him close to her heart, she told her friend, Pauline Boulanger, and

Pauline was friends with my sister, Rachel, who loved to blabber with almost everyone, myself included for I was her little sister.] *Un jour, on les a pris, Rosa et Jean, derrière la clôture de la petite prairie de Monsieur Fuseau à s'étreindre comme deux enfants gauches dans leur embarras d'affection. C'est Rosa, nous dit-on, qui avait pris l'avance et qui avait donné un petit baiser à Jean qui resta un peu saisi de gêne et d'embarras. Elle était garçonnière à sa façon, Rosa Bonheur, mais elle n'hésitait pas de suivre les impératifs du coeur lorsque l'envie lui prenait, je vous mens pas.* [One day, they were caught behind the fence of the Mister Fuseau's little prairie holding on to one another like two children, a bit awkward in their embarassment of the display of affection. It was Rosa who had taken the first step, we were told, and she had given poor Jean a little kiss who stood there somewhat taken aback with astonishment and embarassment. She was a bit of a tomboy, Rosa was, but she did not hesitate following the impulses of her heart when they took a hold of her, I'm not lying.] *Je sais que vous ne me croirez pas parce que ce n'est pas la Rosa que vous avez connue, mais elle était jeune en ce temps-là, et puis elle ne voulait pas contrarier ses impulsions, je crois bien. Elle était humaine comme toute jeune fille. Elle finit par mettre court à ses petites affections pour le jeune homme, car Jean lui-même a abandonné tout signe d'amitié et d'affection pour la jeune fille de seize ans, Rosa Bonheur. On ne sait pas pourquoi, mais on se doute des implications d'amour naissant chez les deux, surtout du jeune homme qu'on appelait Jean Leiderer. Si Rosa Bonheur en a parlé plus tard, je n'en sais rien. Seulement que la Rosa Bonheur que moi j'ai connue, elle cachait dans son coeur de femme une affection pour un jeune homme, artiste en herbe lui-même, qui ne pouvait pas échanger tangiblement l'affection avec une jeune fille. Il ne s'est jamais marié. C'est un moment dans la vie de Rosa Bonheur qui demeure caché et enseveli dans la mémoire de l'artiste que l'on connaît comme artiste connue et admirée par tous ses amis et connaissances.* [I know that you will not believe me because it's not the Rosa Bonheur that everyone knows, but she was young then and she did not want to contradict her impulses, I believe. After all, she was as human as all other girls are. She eventually put an end to her little affections for the young man, for Jean himself had abandoned all signs of friendship and affection for the young sixteen year old girl, Rosa Bonheur. We do not know why, but we have doubts about the implications of a budding love affair between both of them especially on the part of the young man we called Jean Leiderer. If Rosa Bonheur talked about this affair later on, I know nothing of it. Only that the Rosa Bonheur I knew hid in her woman's heart an affection for a young man, a budding artist himself, who could not share tangibly the affection of a young girl. He never married. It's a moment in Rosa Bonheur's life that remains hidden and buried in the memory of the artist that we know as one who is well known and admired by all her admirers for her great work.] *D'ailleurs, tout le monde connaît l'attachement intime qu'a témoigné Rosa Bonheur envers sa grande amie, Nathalie Micas et l'amour que l'artiste a eu pour Anna l'Américaine jusqu'à la loger chez elle au Chateau de By. Comment ne pas se soupçonner d'affaires sournoises et souverainement cachées...*Furthermore, everyone knows the very close attachment that Rosa Bonheur manifested toward her intimate friend, Nathalie Micas, and the love that the artist had for Anna Klumpke the American, as far as keeping her home at the Chateau de By. How not to wonder about these suspicious and sovereingly hidden affairs]

"*Une minute,* wait a doggone minute there, *Mademoiselle Clairdomaine, Rosa Bonheur fut et demeure ma très grande amie et je l'ai toujours connue chaste et franche dans ses relations avec moi. Nous étions tous deux des artistes vouées à l'art. Rien ne s'est passé que l'on pourrait indiquer comme sexuel. Rien. Rosa Bonheur était un modèle de femme énergique et capable de démontrer de l'affection pour une amie sans gêner du tout la relation entre elle et l'autre. Je l'admirais grandement Rosa Bonheur et je lui portais mon admiration et, oui, mon amour, car je la considérais ma héroïne dans les arts et par sa tenue comme artiste de conséquence. Toute son affection humaine fut coulée dans son attachement aux animaux qu'elle considérait souvent plus humains que les humains même...*Just a minute there, Mademoiselle Clairdomaine, for Rosa Bonheur was and rermains my very good friend and I have always known her to be chaste and frank in her relationship with me. We were both of us artists devoted to art. Nothing transpired that could be taken as sexual. Nothing. Rosa Bonheur was the model of an energetic woman and capable of demonstrating affection for a friend without hampering at all the relationship between each one. I admired her greatly, Rosa Bonheur, and I offered her my admiration and my affection becasuse I considered her to be my heroine in the arts and by her reputation as an artist of consequence. All of her human affection was channeled into the animals that she often considered to be more human than the humans themselves]."

Miss Clairdomaine took leave of Anna Klumpke and the others saying that she could not compete with educated people, and that she did not want to confront Rosa Bonheur about the issue of love and affection. All she wanted to do, she said before leaving for the spheres beyond, was that she wanted to open up Rosa Bonheur's life as a woman and as a budding artist that nobody knew about. Rosa Bonheur herself had long gone to her resting place in the spheres and so did the Empess Eugénie who did not want to get involved with such petty matters. Anna Klumpke remained for she had the task of continuing the story as delineated by the author himself. After all, he needed, I needed, someone to finish what I had started, a novel on Rosa Bonheur's life and works. I could not do it myself. I could but I would have sounded inauthentic and boring.

CHAPTER SIX

Now is the time and place to render homage to Rosa Bonheur's art and the full impact of her talent in the world of art and art admirers, and, I might add, of critics too. An artist does not need a critic to get a stamp of approval for his and her works of art, but a critic does play a role in the artist's life as a lightning rod or a litmus test of the artist's work. Critics are like little children who go about tasting bonbons and selecting those they really like and discarding those they dislike, sometimes being very vocal about their choices. They extoll those they favor and condemn those they reject according to their taste in art. In the art world, there are some paintings thats critics do not like and give them a bad press, while the public's stance, at times, is just the opposite of the critic's choice. However, along comes a painting that meets both the critic's and the public's taste and choice, like Rosa Bonheur's "The Horse Fair." We've already talked about this fine work, or I should say Rosa Bonheur did, and we need not elaborate any longer on this splendid work of art. As the author of this novel, I would like to bring back Anna Klumpke who knew Rosa Bonheur and her entire work better than many others to talk to us about Rosa Bonheur's paintings and their esthetic values. After all, Anna Klumpke was an artist on her own right and a fine painter she was. I refer to two of her paintings, "Portrait of Rosa Bonheur" and "Catinou Knitting." Besides, she too was awarded the Legion of Honor by the French government in 1924.

Now, now there is no need to extoll my reputation as artist and woman since my life and my work speak for themselves as they do for Rosa

Bonheur. I have admired her ever since I was a child. I even had a Rosa Bonheur doll. That's how popular she was. She had a doll made after her just like Shirley Temple. I loved my doll and always wished to meet the artist some day. And, I did. However, I'm not back here on earth to talk about myself but I've been given the beautiful and generous task of presenting in detail several of Rosa Bonheur's paintings that made her internationally famous.

First, let's begin with a painting that was inspired by a visit to the Highlands in England while Rosa Bonheur was visiting this country with her friend, Nathalie Micas. She had been urged to travel there by Ernest Gambart, her agent. He felt that she needed a rest and a trip to get away from her everyday chores and work. She needed new and different inspiration levels, and he urged her to travel to another country, one that he knew very well, England. She not only traveled to England but eventually landed in Scotland. I did not know her then, but I can give you a detailed description of a painting that she called " The Charcoal Burners" [*Les Charbonniers*]. She got her inspiration while in Scotland. Charcoal making is not an easy task. It's a matter of putting wood in a huge pit and setting fire to the wood until it is carbonized. That takes a long time, but the process yields chacoal. It must have been an arduous task for the charcoal burners, and Rosa Bonheur was fascinated by it all. She took copious notes and her memory, which was an astounding one for keeping details and storing colors, allowed her to produce imagery and visual perceptions that became an eventual painting. She did have a keen mind and a sense of imaging things with her intellectual prowess. That I know since I lived with her for ten years and worked alongside her while in the *atelier*.

Here is the painting of "The Charcoal Burners" as I view it. There's a pair of oxen attached to a two-wheel cart in the very center of it. In the cart there is a full load of carbonized wood, huge black chunks, while a man holds onto a large pile of charcoal. He has climbed up a small ladder to reach his work product. He has a beard, wears a dark blue shirt over which he wears some kind of apron, probably made out of reddish leather. On his head, we see a white kerchief of some kind. There's another man to the left side, and he wears gray trousers and a white shirt. He is raking some charcoal, but we cannot see his face since he has his back turned to the viewer. In the background, one can see trees and their foliage with glimpses of a blue sky and some passing clouds. Smoke is rising from the pit and hovers around the head of the man standing next to the cart. The ground is full of debris of rocks and pieces of wood with tufts of green leaves here and there. There is some kind of a mound wood a bit afar, stacked as if in a pyramid.

What truly fascinates me are the two oxen in full view, right in the viewer's face and eyes, the one who is looking at and admiring these two beasts of burden. They're amazing animals because the artist has expertly reproduced them with a sharp and magnificent adroitness and a fine sense of realism. They are both cream-colored with beautiful horns that stick out of heir heads. Their faces and eyes are fixed straight ahead as if ready to pull the cart to its destination. Their noses are wet to the touch, if one could do so. That's how real their noses are. The front hooves are well delineated. One can really see that these beasts of burden are truly strong, muscular and magnificent animals. Rosa Bonheur knew exactly what she was doing here and displayed her keen sense of *animalière*. The light color of both beasts harmonizes with the natural light that shines directly on them, while the black charcoal serves as a dark contrast. I know that the painting is more than the focus on animals with the two men in the scene as charcoal burners, but the main focal point, I believe, are the two animals. The two oxen await their charge as beasts of burden, and are therefore the center of the activity in this painting. Rosa Bonheur knew that they would be the main focal point and that the chore of charcoal burning would become subsidiary to it. I think it's a splendid work of art inspired from her days in Scotland. It also reminds us of the hard work and toil of both animals and men at a time when charcoal was needed and made by hard-working men with tough animals by their side. The painting is a reflection of the working man's place in society and the needs he meets and fulfills.

The next painting is called "Changing of Meadow" [*Changement de Pâturages*]. Of course, I am being selective here just because there are so many of Rosa Bonheur's paintings that one must choose some and leave others behind. You will have to follow my taste, dear reader. I lead the project and therefore I'm fulfilling my task as delineator and describer of the paintings I select. You just will have to bear with me in the selection of paintings. After all, I too am an artist. I know and recognize true art when I see it, although I have no problems with Rosa Bonheur's works of art. I may be a bit prejudiced, but the whole world recognizes her ability to render recognizable and realisitc art at its highest degree of esthetics.

"Changing of Meadow" is a painting that delights me and my sense of light and color since the entire atmosphere here is of natural light and pastel colors. It delights me and rejuvenates me since I always loved sunlight and light colors. They resonate well in my heart of liveliness and warmth. It's livley because light throws *la vie* into everything and it's warm because of its quality of the sun's rays warming your skin and bones. It certainly warms the sheep here in the *chaloupe* . The scene is the Scottish Highlands. Here we have a boatload of sheep being displaced from one meadow to another. But the other meadow is far away across the river so that the sheep have to be transported by boat. It's quite a boatload we have here. The sheep are all crowded together head to head and bodies upon bodies of wool stuck to one another, so that the whole boatload appears to be nothing but sheep with heads bobbing here and there as if each sheep is trying to breathe air the best it can. We can see white heads as well as a few black ones in the crowded mêlée of sheep.They must be wondering where they are going and what caused their displacement. A lack of *pâturage,* of grazing in a meadow filled with green grasses that have been depleted by constant grazing by hungry if not voracious sheep.

There are three men in the boat, two young ones and an older man with long white hair. The two young men are rowing, each one with a long oar. They both have bright red curly hair.The older man sits at the back of the boat gazing forward. All three are wearing dark green tams. The older one wears a dark green shirt or possibly a light coat with a tartan plaid scarf hanging from his right shoulder which hangs on the back of the boat practically touching the water. Up ahead, another boatload of sheep is being carted away to another meadow. There are only two men in this one, each one of them rowing. The boat is made of sturdy weathered wood. The two boats are headed toward a peninsula of land of some kind, not too far away. The background scene is of mountains and hazy skies with enough sunlight to brighten the boatload of sheep in the foreground. The waters are choppy green with blue shades done by the masterful brushstrokes of an artist who knows her craft very well, enough to make the waters realistic and esthetically remarkable. As one of the rowers dips his long oar into the water, we can see the water dripping from the oar which makes us realize that the artist has given us a scene of rapturous pastel colors of water and bright light in a way to heighten the slow and delibertate movement of a boatload of sheep on the waters. Overall, it's a magnificent painting that reveals Rosa Bonheur's skill as an artist and a keen observer of shepherds dealing diligently with their sheep and their pasturing. Her *animalière* tendency is truly revealed here for we are indeed struck by the boatload of crammed sheep being transported to another pasture. The sheep are the true focus here.

As much as I like Rosa Bonheur's paintings of the Scottish Highlands, I have to move on to another time and another scene, that of horses. This one is called "Wild Horses"[*Chevaux sauvages*]. Before I begin with the horses and this particular painting, I want to say this, that Rosa Bonheur cared for all creatures and she loved them over the span of sixty tears whether they came from the plains or the mountains, the forest or the African desert, whether domestic animals or wild beasts. She showed her love for all of them in a very special way and they returned her favor, for she deeply believed that animals have souls and can love back and show their affection in some ways that she, Rosa Bonheur, understood so very well. As for horses, I found among her papers this meditaion, and I will quote it to you for I find that it is truly worth giving it to you word for word: "Like man, the horse is the most beautiful or the most wretched of creatures. Yet man becomes ugly and shameful through vice or poverty; he is almost responsible for his decadence. The horse, on the other hand, is just a slave that the Creator entrusted to man and which man abuses in his ingratitude and cowardly, selfish wretchedness, even to the point of making himself lower than the most brutish beast." I must say that these are strong even harsh words on her part, for Rosa Bonheur was not in the habit of doing so. She was a mild-hearted woman. Apparently, she had a very ardent love of horses and saw too many things in her lifetime that prompted her to meditate and write down her thoughts on the horse with such ardor, if not fury, when it comes to man's abuse of animals, especially of horses. It just had to be said, I suppose, and I agreed with her.

Now, "Wild Horses". In the very center of this painting, stands erect and powerfully strong in stance and in muscular appearance, a chestnut-colored horse with a very shiny coat that resonates well with the artistic approach of the master painter. Rosa Bonheur loved horses so much that she could not help herself in revealing the true and frank expression of her esthetic equine fascination. Here we have a wild horse, quite possibly from the Camargue, for there are not too many *chevaux sauvages* roaming in France. The artist has focused on this particular steed while there are several others in the background, grazing. The horse is standng erect on green pasture with a background of blue sky and cumulus clouds, and the light of the sun giving the horse bright and glossy touches of chestnut color on the shoulder, the flank, the belly, and the right thigh. The face has glimmers of light especially shown above the nostrils. His gaze is straight and seemingly determined. His flowing mane is jet black as well as his long tail hanging down. He is ready for the wild jaunt into freedom, a free-spirited animal is he, for he has earned the right to wildness and freedom that a horse favors over domesticity. He is standing still as if in a pose for the artist which is indeed a formidable occasion for the master painter, the artist, Rosa Bonheur, to capture equine wildness in quiet and motionless stance. Of course, the artist can do whatever she wants to given the fact that her memory serves her well, and she has all the time she needs to reproduce this beautiful animal on canvas. I am sure that she relished this memory of a wild horse in his peaceful element standing strong and majestic just the way horses are in Rosa Bonheur's mind. Rosa Bonheur has rendered here a glorious rendition of wildness at peace in nature that reflects her deep love of horses. I liked horses but I did not love them as Rosa Bonheur did. Hers was a genuine love for the creatures of the Creator, as she used to tell me so very often.

Now comes a painting whose inspiration was the Pyrenees and a topical feature that is called transhumance. This is the moving of livestock from the farms in the valleys up to the higher grounds of the mountains for the summer months. Transhumance took the form of a biannual mass migration moving uphill in May or June and returning to the farms in September or October. The Pyrenees are flat-topped massifs and it's range is enormous. The mountains provide the farmers relief from both the heat of the sun and the dryness of the climate as well as offering new and fresher grazing grounds for animals such as sheep and cows. This is what Rosa Bonheur told me about the Spanish side of the Pyrenees and its farmer-shepherds. The title of the painting is "Shepherd of the Pyrenees" [*Berger des Pyrénées*]. I truly like this painting because it reflects the peace and harmony of a scene in nature that Rosa Bonheur treasured.

One seemingly lonely shepherd sits on a large rock up in the mountain. He sits alone surrounded by some of his sheep who have come up to him and gaze at him while he remains quiet and apparently unattentive, except to cradle the muzzle of one of the sheep with his right hand. The mountains are surrounded with heavy clouds that seem to touch and envelop the three peaks that are shown. There is filtered light on the scene. Tree stumps and jagged elongated bare tall remnants of trees jut out of the grassy and rocky ground. There are huge rocks, boulders here and there, making the area looking like a deserted land. The shepherd is looking forward while his sheep are wanting his attention. All are white wool sheep with the exception of two black ones. There are a dozen or so sheep around the shepherd. He knows his sheep and his sheep know him much like the gospel shepherd, one might say. Caring and the love of his animals are the characteristics of this good and faithful shepherd. Tiny white flowers are sprinkled here and there resembling the white blossom of the Alps, the eidelweis, the symbol of alpinism. Even they seem lonely but faithful so far up. It's a quiet spot, a solace from a hard climb and away from the noise of the villages below.

The shepherd is wearing a large flat brown Basque beret, a jacket of some kind and a blue shirt underneath with reddish-orange touches. He has brown leggings with well-polished boots. The shepherd holds a long staff in his left hand, more like a pole with the top resting on his left shoulder. The mood is pensive, meditative and serene, somewhat reminiscent of Jean-François Millet's painting of the "Angelus." The artist has created this mood with colors, and brushstrokes that imitate the mood of the caring, ever faithful and daring shepherd keeping his flock high up in the mountains of the Pyrenees. Rosa Bonheur has succeeded in her artistic efforts to render the quality and strength of her *animalière* propensities with her indulgence for people like the shepherds who complement the animals they shepherd and care for. It takes great devotion and personal skill to be a shepherd much like those that Rosa Bonheur brings to her paintings. As to the first visit to the Pyrenees, Rosa Bonheur accompanied by her friend Nathalie Micas, both enjoyed their climb in the mountains. Nathalie recounts to her mother that although she wanted to accomplish a pilgrimage to Lourdes, the visionary site, she was unable to do it due to a fever that she had. She and Rosa Bonheur had to go to another site, a place where the warm waters would help to heal their physical malaise, at Ems.

We have explored horses and sheep so far in Rosa Bonheur's paintings, and now I would like to talk about other animals painted by Rosa Bonheur such as "The Fox"*[Le renard]*. This painting is a very simple portrayal of a fox in surroundings of tall grasses. It's a very realistic view of the animal, and Rosa Bonheur shows here not only her love of animals but her deliberate and dedicated affection for wild animals such as the fox. It's a beautiful animal what with its gorgeous tail and its fur that capture the essence of the fox. The artist pictures him as if *aux aguets*, watchful and hesitant, with his eyes on the beholder, glaring and full of apprehension. After all, it is a wild animal so very often fearful of the human presence. I really like this painting because it reveals Rosa Bonheur's astute skill of reproducing a live animal in nature with all of its qualities and natural beauty.

Two long black legs emerge from the front of the fox, steady on the green moss. His bushy tail with a white fluffy tip is curled around him. His long brownish coat of fur glows in certain spots and his two upright triangular ears perked up as if to hear better any impending sounds. His snout is elongated and pointed slightly upward with a black shiny nose. He sits next to sprays of long glistening green grasses that serve as a backdrop to the painting. There is a deep dark presence of some kind in the far right corner contrasting the glowing light of the tall grasses. I cannot make out what it is. These green tall grasses give the painting a kind of ethereal glow that seemingly soothes the apprehension and possible dismay of the poor animal who appears to be fearful of the entire situation at hand. The artist has truly captured the beauty of the fox as well as the wildness that surrounds a fox such as this one. I'm sure this painting was not done *in situ* but the artist's reproduction of her seeing a fox like this one is vivid and memorable. Her memory is simply astounding when it comes to animals in the wild and, of course, with other animals that are tame and domesticated. Rosa Bonheur had a passion for animals and a rage for work and the two combined to produce marvelous works of art.

Having talked about a fox out in the wild of the woods, I want to proceed with a domesticated animal and a very cute one at that, a white lamb. As a matter of fact, Rosa Bonheur painted the head of one sticking out of tall grasses. It's a marvelous painting that I admire and love very much since I do have a fondness for white lambs. This one is simply enthralling as far as I'm concerned. It has all the qualities of a tender, pure and I-want-to-cuddle-you type of lamb. His eyes are all aglow, wide and sparkling in the morning sunlight. It's title is "Head of Lamb" [*Tête d'agneau*]. The painting is a simple yet appealing lamb's head. It's the simplicity of it that makes it so enthralling in my view of things.

Here we see a lamb's head jutting out of green grasses swallowing up the entire body of the young lamb except its head as if to escape the sea of grasses. The soft white fleece emerges in the light of day while the muzzle of the lamb is held upward as if smelling the breeze in the air. However, what fascinates one is the tender blueish gray look in his eye, the left one that we see, ever so enchanting and inviting to the one who is viewing this art work. One just cannot ignore the simplcity of the head with its eye reflecting the innocence of the white lamb. It's a fascinating thing, this eye of the lamb. The green grasses serve as a background and foreground of this particular painting. They're lush and bright green grasses. The head of this lamb becomes a clear and evident testimony of Rosa Bonheur's love of animals be they horses, oxen, foxes or sheep. Lambs not unlike foals and calves ever endearing to those who love the young of any animal. *Tête d'agneau* is thus a product of the artist's brushstrokes and choice of colors that do not belie her sense of radiant beauty in the love of animals by a true *animalière*. Sheep, I mean ewes and rams, are likeable and worthy of our delight but lambs are totally endearing and sweet to one's taste for innocent creatures who invite all of us to cherish and delight in their innocence and their rapture. Lamb of God have mercy on all creatures who abide by you and the stars in heaven. Lambs get lost very easily and that's the reason why shepherds must be vigilant and faithful to their charge of shepherding, day and night, lest the wolves come and devour them. I cannot help myself saying beware of wolves dressed in sheep's clothing. That's a bit too cliché if not corny, I might add. Rosa Bonheur would laugh at this bit of a cautionary proverb.

Next come the dogs in my list of paintings by Rosa Bonheur. Dogs are friendly, faithful, intelligent and affectionate animals. Rosa Bonheur loved dogs and was always surrounded by some dog be it her Tayo, her Blue and

Tan King Charles Spaniel, or her Barbaro. She did many paintings of dogs that were thought of as minor works, but I myself do not consider them minor. They're not grandiose like the "Horse Fair" but they are important in the long list of paintings by Rosa Bonheur. She had a special affection for her dogs, for all dogs just like she had a very special affection for horses. Every single animal, for her, had its individual personality and each one had its own characteristics. Such was the case for Pierrette, Fathma, and Tayon. Pierrette was a favorite animal of hers, a lioness who was born in the circus. She was affectionate and kind. That beast was something else, said Rosa Bonheur. She also raved about her tenderness with other animals. Pierette used to let a cat eat its supper between her paws without budging. That lioness liked playing hide-and-seek with the horse and donkey that grazed in the meadow. She would dash back and forth up to them, woofing like a dog at play. On the other hand, Fathma was cuddly and more affectionate than Pierrette. She followed her mistress like a poodle. In her frolics, she often made a mess of things. She was forgiven easily and all of the time without a single reproach. She was a model of obedience and docility to a point that she let Rosa put her paws arround her neck without ever scratching her or doing any harm to her neck and face. Rosa Bonheur cried when she found Fathma dead, one day, at the foot of the stairs. She did not sob deliberately but I could see that it pained her to tell me about it. Rosa Bonheur was such a tender-hearted woman when it came to animals. I may add that she was the same way with people with whom she had managed to weave a strong attachment. Friendship was above all the strength of the chords of her attachment and inevitable love as a woman. The bond of friendship was strong and indelible for both people she cared for and the animals she so cherished.

Besides the lionesses, Pierrette and Fathma, Rosa Bonheur favored certain dogs although she loved all the dogs that came her way one way or another. I remember that one day she found a poor little creature of a dog that was caught in the brambles of a wild bush near the Fontainebleau forest. She told me that it was almost impossible to retrieve the poor animal without hurting herself and the poor dog. She wandered around the bush until she decided to stick her arm into the brambles without even a single cry from her mouth. She felt the hurt of the thorny branches but she did not give up on loosening the dog from its branches. The little dog whimpered and seemed to beg her to be careful with him, and she did so without hurting the little creature. She later felt the excruciating pain of being scratched deeply on her two arms but the pain was mollified by the feeling of kindness and mercy that she had exercised that afternoon. She named the little dog, Safran, after the orangy spice that she loved so very much in her food when Céline brought her supper once in a while. The cook liked to experiment with various ethnic foods. Céline was a friend of hers from the neighborhood. Unfortunately, little Safran liked to wander and especially go hunting in the forest. He chased small wild animals and mice. One day, he never returned. Rosa found his torn collar and the medal with his name on it. No dog. She dreaded the truth of her little Safran devoured by some wild animal for the forest was deep and forbidding. She lamented Safran for a while until she met another little dog that was ambling along on the edge of the woods near the Chateau de By. He had been attracted by her own little dog named *"Peluche noir"* a dog that had been given to her by one of the villagers of Thomery. One of these villagers had surnamed Rosa Bonheur, *"La mère aux chiens"* mother of dogs. She was indeed a mother to all dogs and a mother to most animals that she encountered on her path in life. She was, as I named her, *"L'animalière par excellence et la douce mère des animaux sauvages et domestiqués."* She was indeed the sweet mother of both wild and domesticated animals.

As for the painting of Toya, the dog's head is very much up close and it appears to be very casual and straightforward. Tayo was a white and tan dog with large floppy ears that were completely tan in color. His mouth was slightly opened, his large nose was wet most of the time, and his fur not very long with hairs sticking out here and there. There were especially long tall hairs on the bridge of his nose close to his right eye. What was most remarkable about Tayo were his eyes, his soft brown eyes. His gaze was straight and somewhat melancholic. Here in the painting, he shows no sign of endearment or apprehension, not even of attachment to its owner. Rosa Bonheur painted him in a mood of utter indifference, it seems, but not of utter disdain. Tayon was a good dog but not one you could get close to enough to cuddle, embrace and give him kisses when the urging was there. Rosa Bonheur did not care, she so very often gave him some hugs although he backed away somewhat indifferent to her advances. Some dogs are like that.

Brizo, well, he was of another breed. He was a shepherd's dog, a likable, even cuddly sort of a dog. He looks somewhat sad here in the painting or even inconsolable, you might say, because that's the way one sees him. He certainly is not jovial here, not filled with fun and laughter. Brizo's fur is long and sprouts out like tan-yellowish weeds on top of his head. He has long floppy ears that grow somber and darker towards the tips. He has a large wet black nose and his eyes are half hidden beneath the hairs that surround them, so it's difficult to distinguish their color. The fur on his body is a bit tangled and grows from frizzy white to dun tan. Altogether, the dog's fur harmonizes very well with the dark grasses in the background. It's the dog that's the point of focus here. The background is truly a background of little interest since it does not draw our interest. Brizo was a most lovable dog, a shepherd's delight on a long day's journey up the mountain or in a meadow watching over the shepherd's flock. Brizo was a true companion. Rosa Bonheur truly liked him enough to become infatuated with the little creature when he returned her love in so many ways.

On the other hand, the small black and tan dog named, at first, "*L'inconnu*" by the Chateau staff, since he came out of nowhere, and later named ZouZou by Rosa Bonheur, was a charming creature, affable and generous with his love. The King Charles Spaniel was ever a favorite at court, I am told, especially by the children. He was a true pet and an animal worthy of anyone's love and affection. Rosa Bonheur took Zouzou in like so many other strays in her household. She could not resist what she called "lost souls." "Even animals have souls," she used to tell me, "and they're part of an animal's personality, with each one different than the next." Of course, I believed her since she put so much confidence in her beliefs about animals. What else could I do? If you lived with Rosa Bonheur, as long as I have, you begin to adopt her tender approach to animals and their individual qualities. She truly meant what she said about animals being noble in their own right, affectionate if you allow them to love you, faithful in their tenderness, and ever protective of the love you give them. Be they horses, oxen, cows, sheep, birds, or even tiny creatures like beetles, they all have determined qualities that make them individuals as part of nature's scheme. That's the way the Creator had made them, she used to say. That's the way they behave like animals and not like denatured human beings who seek to abuse them. I have always respected her views on animals. Rosa Bonheur was a woman of kindred spirit with each and every animal that she met and had in her menagerie. Let no one betray her confidence in allowing animals to be in their rightful place in nature and in the domesticity that surrounded them.

Zouzou was a small Spaniel as most of them are, and his appearance was one of domestic love and faithfulness while he often claimed his own independence as an animal of a pure bred lineage. Although his fur was indeed black and tan, his overall appearance was one of mixture of colors and fuzziness. I mean that he was not altogether black but had patches of bright tan, while there were large splotches of tan here and there especially around his hind legs. His large eyes mirrored the soulfulness within, as Rosa Bonheur used to say.

The next dog was not Rosa Bonheur's but she wanted to paint his picture for she truly loved this dog. He belonged to a friend of hers, a man known as the Vicomte d'Armaille. The dog was a *Limier Briquet Hound* and worthy of its owner. He loved this dog, a constant companion of his. In this painting, Rosa Bonheur placed the hound in a loyal stance, back straight and eyes attentive to suggest he is watching something, possibly his owner. The tail points upwards in a wagging motion to depict happiness and contentment. Brown and green oils are smudged on the canvas together to create a murky forest, possibly the forest of Fontainebleau. The grass and trees blend together to reveal a natural landscape in which the hound could thrive. White and brown mix show off the lustrous coat. There is a fuzzy structure to the paint that mimics how fur can look. This is a definite testament to Rosa Bonheur's skill in replicating animal anatomy. The hound's eyes are remarkably life-like. They are inquisitive and shimmer with intelligence and alertness. A collar merges with the neck's fur to highlight domesticity. The forest is nature personified and a dog is a byproduct. Man has tamed the wild and the hound is loyal to his human master.

Rosa Bonheur was truly in her glory as an artist when she found the right subject for her painting, and she jumped on the occasion to do so such as this particular hound that she truly loved, although she was not a hunter herself. She loved all kinds of dogs and she reveled in the fact that she could paint whichever one she could come across in her daily life. She was fortunate, for she did come across some really dandy ones. I don't know the name of the Limier hound but that doesn't matter as long as Rosa Bonheur's fame as an artist was veritably enhanced by a work of art such as this one, the work of an *animalière accomplie et renommée.*

59

CHAPTER SEVEN

At this junction, I dare to enter the world of the wild animals, specifically the lions. Rosa Bonheur had an affinity for the big cats, as she called them. She had two favorites, Pierrette and Fathma. These two were her charming domesticated pets. She grieved when they both died, especially Fathma. However, she also had a liking for the lions and the lionesses as seen in the wild. She chose some for her paintings. One of them, or I should say two of them with their cubs, is one of my very favorites.

This painting shows a bold and energetic lion next to a lioness and her cubs. King Lion is lying down next to the lioness with her three cubs close to her belly, asleep, most probably after being nursed. The lion is huge in appearance with a very large mane encircling his imposing head. His ears perk up from his large and bold mane, his eyes gazing earnestly ahead of him, his nose broad, and his muzzle covered with short white hair in a daunting and determined seriousness that only a lion can display. His huge front paws with hidden claws extend from his two strong legs and lie evenly on the bare ground. The lioness lies comfortably next to him with her smooth body stretched out alongside. Her light tan fur is shiny in the natural light of day while there are white areas of her skin, under her muzzle, under her stomach and near her back legs, as well as her underbelly. Her eyes are keenly gazing straight ahead, her nose smaller than the lion's, her mouth in earnest seriousness. She is a bold huntress. The strong paws, one under her front stomach, the other highly exposed while the two back paws, one of which reveals the black pads on which to stalk a prey, and the other on top. Her tail lies over one of her back paws while the long and rugged tail of the lion with its black tail tuff is stretched out behind her. As for the three cubs, they're cute and adorable little creatures much like kittens that we love to cuddle. All three are snuggled in the lap of luxury, the wild luxury of being nursed to contentment, and the luxury of being cared for and protected by the mother lioness. The two of them, the lion and the lioness, captured by the artist in a majestic and regal pose that Rosa Bonheur, the *animalière,* in her ability to render the essence of animal splendor has done with esthetic appeal.

Another animal in the wild painted by Rosa Bonheur is the "Royal Tiger Marching"[*Le Tigre royal*]. The Royal Tiger is also known as the Bengal Tiger and is very often referred to by this name. Rosa Bonheur never saw a tiger in the wild. She must have seen one in a reproduction or in a zoo. I know that she was quite familiar with the Delacroix's lithograph of the Royal Tiger. Delacroix himself had great empathy with the natural world and was fascinated by animals. He never did encounter an untamed one in the wild, so he had to resort to the resources of the Paris zoo. Some say that Delacroix, in this lithograph of the Royal Tiger, demonstrated the Romantic penchant for tragedy, torment, and violence in scenes that showed nature in tooth and claw. In Delacroix' work we see a huge tiger as if crawling on the ground with his eyes wide open to the challenge and trepidation of imminent fury, the fury of the stalking and the kill.

Rosa Bonheur's tiger is more of a large and bold feline on the prowl slowly advancing towards its prey or whatever catches its gaze. There is no torment, no violent premonition and no traumatic event. Just a pose for the artist to consider in her rendering of the natural habitat and the naturalness of the animal.

Here we have a tiger, Royal Tiger or a Bengal Tiger, if you want, in its full colors and stance as a big cat in the jungle, I suppose. The tiger's coat is yellow to light orange with stripes ranging from dark brown to black. The belly and the interior parts of the limbs are white. The tail, orange with black rings. It's a very colorful animal. Rosa Bonheur wanted to capture this animal in her creative but realistic way as an artist-*animalière*. I believe she succeeded very well. I know she did. This Royal Tiger looks majestic and imposing in its stance, and in the way the artist was able to reproduce this essence of the tiger.

Then comes the painting of the "Lion in a Mountainous Landscape" [*Lion dans un paysage montagneux*]. What is most remarkable here is the bushy and flowing long mane of the lion going from the whitish front hair to the tan hair down to the darker brown hair that make up his mane. His head is turned toward the left with eyes staring straight ahead as if to spot the next focus in and around the terrain. The face is boldly delineated with eyes peering through thick fur surrounding them. It's an elongated face, the mouth is closed, the nose distinctly feline with a white tuft of hair hanging from his chin. The overall fur is tan in color except for the long dark hair hanging from his underbelly. We can see his male accountrement right below the stem of his strong elongated tail ending with a tuft of dark hair. His legs and paws are firm, thick and solidly planted on the ground he stands. We can tell that the claws that are hidden from view are enormous. He's a regal and majestic beast of the wild. He's an animal of power and strength. It's easy to detect in his enormous power as a lion that he is indeed king of the realm. Gazing at him we can readily say that we are awaiting his roar so vividly realistic portrayed by the skilled artist that is Rosa Bonheur with animals.

The background is of the mountains imbued with natural light and given the hues of the pastel colors blending in with the cloudless sky above. There are two ranges of mountains, one above and one below, the darker one. The one filled with the shadows of the day of deeper color. The expanse is huge, wide and seemingly endless. Here Rosa Bonheur has truly captured the majesty not only of the mountains but also of the animal in nature, the living and imposing lion for he stands like an icon before us who are enthralled with his supreme presence. I just stand here before such a painting and am reminded of the artistic skill of the painter Rosa Bonheur, my friend and teacher.

At this point, I must bring in the paintings of the smaller animals that Rosa Bonheur painted. She did so many paintings that sometimes I'm confused by her diligence in reproducing so many outstanding works of art that heave borne her signature and her mark on the history of painting. I want to talk about some of my very favorites like the calf's head, the wildcat, the doe and her fawn. The calf's head is a lovely reproduction of the head of a calf with the expression of a dear one who is sheltered and cared for. I just cannot put that expression out of my mind seeing the soleful very large dark eyes bulging, I would say, and the wet nose and big nostrils. The calf has wide open ears with tufts of white hair in his right ear and darker hairs in the left one. The calf's hair is of a cream-tan color. He has a doleful expression with a dark and deep look in his eyes. He is gazing straight at you as if to beg for some quite attention. You feel as if you want to touch his head and caress it . You might want to give him a bottle of milk so as to nurse him, but I'm sure he's been already thoroughly weaned. It's a picture of innocence in the animal world. Most of the cows and their calves were, of course, domesticated, and Rosa Bonheur knew most of them in our neighborhood of Thomery.

Now, I want to describe the painting of the wild cat, *le Chat Sauvage*. He's not a big cat, certainly not as big as a lion or a tiger, but somewhat larger than a house cat. He is *sauvage* and can be quite wild most of the time. Be careful how to approach him, told me Rosa Bonheur, although she was never really afraid of wild animals. She knew how to approach them with love, respect and care. She always had the qualities of handling animals respectfully. They all had their very own personalities, she would say, and one has to respect that. She was adamant about this. This one here is a wildcat lying down with his body stretched out on the mossy ground. He looks like a domesticated cat, but he is not one. Wildcats have been known to be fierce and unpredictable. He is lying down on his right side, his head is elevated and his eyes are gazing in front of him whatever may be out there. His nose and his ears are perked up. His fur is of a light tan color with some white hair beneath his chin. Black fur runs down his back and down to his long bushy tail where there are two black rings towards the black tuft at the every end of it. This cat looks peaceful and seems to be resting there. It's a beautiful animal and Rosa Bonheur has captured the naturalness and the beauty of the beast called the wildcat. She loved all beasts big and small, even lizards and beetles as well as the tiniest ant crawling around. "They're all there for a purpose," she used to say, "and I do not begrudge their appearance in my big and sumptuous menagerie that is the Creator's menagerie. He created it for us humans to enjoy and learn from each and everyone of such creatures. We are creatures of God too since we share the entire creation and the earth with them. We must learn to appreciate each and everyone of these beasts and animals because we are here on earth with them and they are here with us. They were created to give us comfort and a sense of belonging. They belong to us and we belong to them. We're all in the same boat, a gigantic Noah's Ark."

At this precise juncture, I will pass you readers and witnesses to Rosa Bonheur's life and work to Ernest Gambart, Rosa Bonheur's agent and sort of confidant. He worked diligently with her for her many paintings and arranged deals for her. They had a few quarrels but not serious ones, none that I know anything about. I'll let him talk about himself and about Rosa Bonheur. He loved talking about himself. You won't find him here in this sphere for he was relegated to a lower level for whatever reason God chose based on Monsieur Gambart's merit in life. Besides, I've been at it for too long a time right now. I shall return when the proper time comes. Aurevoir and certainly not ADIEU.

CHAPTER EIGHT

My name is Jean Joseph ErnestTheodore Gambart and history calls me a Belgian-born English art publisher and dealer who dominated the London art world in the middle of the nineteenth century, the century in which Rosa Bonheur flourished as an artist/*animalière*. I am here to talk to you about Rosa Bonheur and her art as well as my dealings with her paintings. I was a powerful agent to her and she realized that when I made deals that no one could make for her, and those deals brought her money, the money she used to enjoy life and her freedom to paint and go wherever she wanted.

I moved to Paris when I was nineteen where I established my own print and papermaking business. I soon became known to the well-established Goupil print publishers for whom I moved to England to establish a branch in London. Then I went on my own, this time in partnership with a Mr. Junin to form a company called Gambart & Junin which specialized in the import of prints from Europe. I gained a reputation as a leading publisher of fine arts prints. I established fair and mutually beneficial agreements with most of the best known British and European artists of the time including Edwin Landseer, J.M.W. Turner, Dante Gabriel Rossetti, and, of course, Rosa Bonheur. I helped establish a reputation for many of my clients and Rosa Bonheur was certainly one of them. She needed help and I was there to lend her some very needed assistance in making her work not only noticed but appreciated by a clientele that would pay her substantial sums of money for her works of art. That's when she truly estanlished her career as an *animalière* . I was the one who brought Rosa Bonheur to

England with the monumental work "Horse Fair" that I purchased and which ended up as a private showing for Queen Victoria at Windsor Castle. I also arranged a sojourn to Scotland where Rosa Bonheur made sketches for later works. Through my efforts, she became better known in England than in her native France.

Before you get to know of my misfortunes when I was but nineteen, I will tell you myself about the situation in my young life. I got caught up with a gang of counterfeiters who enticed me to partake of their schemes. I was young then and did not realize what I was doing. I was caught by the police while the others fled. I received a jail sentence of eight years with forced labor, and I was sent to the pilory. That truly humiliated me and my family back in Belgium. I decided then and there never to rely on others for business decisions, money and negotiations. I realized at that point that I had a uncontrolled hunger for success and money that steered me the wrong way. After all, I was an honest man who slipped up occasionally, but this time I had a mess on my hands and I deeply regretted it. I did get out of this mess and claimed my righteous place in the business world. That's where Goupil came into the picture. They were always looking for ways of promoting works of art and providing them at a lower cost as well as making them accessible to the public at large. I worked diligently with the Goupil enterprise and merited their respect and consideration for me and my work, I must say. After ten years of hard work and applied learning about works of art and their sales values, and with the help of Goupil, branches were established in Berlin and in New York City. I was very proud of my involvement in this venture. I always was on the lookout for new and modern means of engraving and lithography. I became the best known seller of engravings. I got up into the world and established a fine reputation. I got invited to many socials and several openings of art works. I not only worked my way into the social world but I also did it with flair and my style of entertaining people. I was a good storyteller and a good *raconteur* . It's true that I was accused sometimes of being a bit daring and *vaniteux*, as they said, but I managed to fit in so that my reputation as an art dealer grew by leaps and bounds. Some said that I was crafty in my business dealings but that I had a genuine and sincere talent in matters of business.

I must say, and without overstating this, that I defended the artistic doctrine in vogue, "*Vérité de la Nature*". Like many of the art dealers in the know, I did not appreciate the Impressionists and their flowery and seemingly unfinished if not melancholic art. I appreciated truth in painting, as they say. Show me a realistic work of art and I will show you a true artist. Show me what is real and not imagined. Show me the works of a Rosa Bonheur who dared to live the working life of men and their animals, and I will show you an artist who is true to her craft. Ah, Rosa Bonheur, what an artist. Her rendition of animals in the flesh and in the real, as I would say it, is marvelous art. Domesticated or wild, her animals have life and "trueness" to them, and that's what sells, I'll have you know. Rosa Bonheur became my friend and I served her well. I took her to places she would have never considered such as England and Scotland. I had her meet people she never would have encountered if it had not been for me. She met Edwain Landseer, the great animal painter of England and they quickly became friends and developed a mutual admiration for each other. Ah, yes, *l'animalier* meets *l'animalière* and they got to share their feelings about art to a point that rumors started going around that Landseer so admired Rosa Bonheur that he wanted to propose marriage to her, he the intolerable and confirmed bachelor. All of this started with his telling Rosa Bonheur, one day, that he suggested that he would be more than happy to become Sir Edwain Bonheur. Can you imagine that? I can't. I couldn't then and I still cannot imagine Sir Edwin Landseer telling that to Rosa Bonheur. She was caught by surprise and did not relish at all the rumors flying around her and Sir Edwin. That people were saying that marriage was in the offing was a great embarrassment to her. I knew that. I tried desperately to squash these rumors but they persisted until Rosa Bonheur disassociated herself from Edwin Landseer. I told Edwin that he should never have said that. He replied that all he meant by his words was that he greatly admired her and her realistic works of art as an *animalière accomplie*. He did not want to marry her or anyone else for that matter. She did not want to marry him or anyone else either. They were not the marrying kind. That led me to think that Rosa Bonheur was an accomplished artist as well as an accomplished maid who thought of marriage as an institution that was intended for those women who failed as an independent person and adhered to society's norms, and I might say rules of behavior. Women were thought of as slaves of the kings's and queens's concept of marriage, that is, considered as totally dependent on men and their desires for sexual appeasement, and especially for begetting an heir, sometimes many offsprings that rendered the woman like a childbearing animal without feelings of her own. Of course, I totally refuse to believe that premise and I would never adhere to slavery of the woman. She had her place in society and she deserved to stay in her place since she was destined by fate to remain a woman and to follow the dictates of society that had been adhered to for centuries. Not a slave, absolutely not. That was my belief. I heard Rosa Bonheur state once her views on the independence of women and their thinking for themselves, something she repeated to me that she had once said to her students. It went this way, *"Je n'ai aucune patience avec les femmes qui demandent la permission de penser. Laissez les femmes établir leurs droits par de grands et bons travaux, et non par des conventions."* [I have no patience with women who ask permission to think. Let women establish their rights by means of grand and good works, and not according to conventions.] Well, that was her way of thinking and I am somewhat in agreement with her. Of course, I never told her that.

As for Miss Anna Klupmke, I told Rosa Bonheur that I thought that her relationship with Miss Klumpke was very good and beneficial to her art since Miss Klumpke much admired her and inspired her to paint and create great canvases. She was an element of good cheer in Rosa Bonheur's life. Of course, she and I had our little differences, and although I admired Miss Klumpke, I could not stand her stubborness probably because she was an American and American women were that way. It all started when she was doing Rosa Bonheur's portrait and I thought that I could represent her as her agent just as I had done with Rosa Bonheur. She did not like the price that I had put on her painting. She thought it was too low and not in line with her skills as an artist. I really thought that she was a newcomer to painting, an amateur, but she reminded me that she had had acclaim from the Paris Salon and had won praise for her work, and that she was no amateur. She was an accomplished artist. Well, I had *égratiné sa peau* as they say in *mon quartier* and she had not liked it at all. I had rubbed her the wrong way. We never did resolve our relationship problem probably because I could not stand her and she could not appreciate my skills as a businessman. I don't really know. It was all nonesense anyway, for me if not for her. Women are so very strange sometimes. I don't understand women. I had three wives and they all were strange in some way. Rosa Boneur is a bit strange but in a different way. Probaby because she is an artist, an artist of real life and I understand her more than other women. It must be because we both have a penchant for money and success.

In any case, after the gaz explosion in my London residence that I named *Rosenstead,* my career as a merchant of fine arts diminished exacerbated by the financial panic in England. It hit me very hard and I lost money, a lot of it. It is then that I decided to retreat from business. Furthermore, the *Commune de Paris* I considered *une nouvelle déception pour moi.* I could not stand Paris anymore and so I moved to Nice. I bought and stayed in the Palais de Marbre that I named "Les Palmiers." Knowing full well that Rosa Bonheur truly loved lions, I sent her some that she decided to paint. It revived her sense of *créativité animalière,* she wrote to me. That woman was indeed in love with animals. She considered them to have each one a personality that mimicked that of humans and that each one had a soul and could respond in kind with human beings. Think about it, animals with souls and their own personality. Lord in heaven!

After Rosa Bonheur's death which caused me grief and sorrow because she had been my friend for many years, I decided to go to Switzerland and live there where I died in a *fauteuil* siezed by an ailment of the lungs. However, before giving up the spirit, I had decided to pay homage to Rosa Bonheur by paying to have erected a monument to her and her memory as an artist. I was so very proud of this decision. I did everything I could for that woman and she rewarded me by painting enough works of great art that I could sell at very good prices as well as make prints for a public avid of her paintings, but could not afford the originals. You could say that I was satisfying the public's thirst for fine arts. Yes, fine arts was my forte and my way to find happiness and satisfaction with the world and society. I am where I am today because of my contributions to fine arts. It may be a lower sphere but it's a worthy one.

"Amen" says Rosa Bonheur.

CHAPTER NINE

Now it's my turn again, Anna Klumpke. I hope that you liked what Ernest Gambart said even though he did not say anything good about me. He did well by Rosa Bonheur. Monsieur Gambart was a very good businessman and I respect him for that, although I thought that he was a bit shady at times. However, that's all over with and he's well installed where he is, in the lower spheres. I must say that he was somewhat of a misogynist when it came to women in the arts and business. There were some women who were very good in business, but he never acknowleged that. Some men like Monsieur Gambart will never acknowledge the virtues and talents of women who do well in the world, and I hope that someday things will change.

Whatever the case may be with Monsieur Gambart, I must not forget Buffalo Bill Cody. Now there's a showman if there was one. Rosa Bonheur fell for him and his entourage, as well as his American West display of horses and Indians. Several Parisians as well as other French people fell under the sway and lure of the American West and especially the Indians, those red-skin people of olden times who had preserved their way of life as well as their customs and features as a native people. The French were fascinated with them. I suppose it was the mysteriousness and the charm of these people that attracted the white Europeans. I really do not know, but I, for one, was not attracted to them, not even Bill Cody, the magnificent showman, as some called him.

Not unlike her father, Rosa Bonheur was an Americanophile and collected prints and photographs of the Wild West. She estimated that

America was at the forefront of modern civilization because of the Americans' admirably intelligent manner of bringing up their daughters and the respect they had for their women. She very much admired them for that, and she wished, all along, that other civilizations such as the Europeans, especially the French, would follow their example.

As for the red-skin people, *les Peaux-Rouges,* Rosa Bonheur quickly identified with them through the prints and sketches of the famous George Catlin. *Le tout Paris* talked about George Catlin with his troupe of "wild" Indians in Paris after his long and well-received great show in London. He came to Paris with a huge menagerie of animals and one hundred and fifteen Indians counting squaws and papooses, they said. It is no wonder that Rosa Bonheur hurried to the Exposition Universelle de Paris of 1889 to take part in the clamor and hunger for Buffalo Bill Cody's great show. The Paris encampment of Indians at the Exposition was a great attraction for the Parisians as well as other French people who had heard of Buffalo Bill. Rosa Bonheur spent weeks sketching at the encampment, and produced more than seventeen paintings and countless sketches. That was the year that I first met Rosa Bonheur, and what a wonder that was for me, Anna Klumpke the American transplanted in France. For years, I had been a great admirer of Rosa Bonheur, the famous woman artist of her century.

There were posters upon giant posters of Buffalo Bill Cody's show in Paris that attracted thousands of people desiring to take part in this American Wild West show. There was one lithograph that showed a huge buffalo on which was superimposed the medallion of Bill Cody's picture, and with the huge letters of *JE VIENS.* That was enough to allure men, women and children to the Exposition. Most of all, everything about the Wild West show with Buffalo Bill Cody fascinated Rosa Bonheur, *prodigieusement* as she told me with exhuberance.

Two Indians that fascinated Rosa Bonheur were Rocky Bear and Red Shirt. She did several sketches of them and some drawings entitled "Buffalo Hunt." She even invited Buffalo Bill Cody to the Chateau de By, and he relished his visit there. He was so delightful as a guest that Rosa Bonheur stood in awe and delight just seeing her American hero there in her atelier. I still do not know why she was so enthralled with him, but I guess that she had long nursed a desire to be part of the American Wild West and specifically with Buffalo Bill Cody. I certainly admired him but was not the least bit enthralled by him, and certainly not enamored of him as Rosa Bonheur was. The American in me did not jump to an overwhelming admiration of the "wild" man who loved horses, buffalos and Indians enough to conjure up a traveling spectacle across the ocean. *L'affaire américaine qui enjôle la populace parisienne,* I called it. This American thing that bewitched the Parisian populace. Rosa Bonheur was so enchanted with the Wild West that she asked me to gather some sagebrush in order to complete the painting of wild horses fleeing a prairie fire. And so, I did it just to please her. On my way westward one day, I got off a train stop to rush and pick up some sagebrush which pleased to no end my artist friend, Rosa Bonheur.

Buffalo Bill Cody truly enraptured the delight of Rosa Bonheur as well as her skills as a painter that were put to very good use in her painting of the showman and his horse. We see here in the painting of Buffalo Bill, a man standing tall in the saddle with his horse, some called Tucker. The horse is trotting. He's an all white mustang of sorts. His two ears are perked up and his eyes big and dark are looking straight ahead. His tail is long and bushy, and flows in the breeze. He is indeed a proud steed much like his master who is looking sideways. Wild Bill has a thick mustache and a goatee with his dark hair flowing over his shoulders. He wears a broad-rim tan hat and buckskins attire with leather gloves, as well as tall black boots. Rosa Bonheur's rendition of Buffalo Bill Cody looks very proud, an attitude very much his trade, I must say. He sits tall in the saddle, as I have said, and evokes an air of superiority if not regal in the pride and self-confidence as a showman of great talent and skill. It is no wonder that Rosa Bonheur felt that she simply had to paint the picture of one of her heroes.

Coming back to my first encounter with Rosa Bonheur, I must tell you of my first impression of her that I carried in my heart and in my mind over the years. From my subtle eye as an artist I could see that Rosa Bonheur was of small stature and well proportioned. She had delicate hands and small feet. Under a high and full forehead, between two arches of eyebrows, one sees the wrinkle that characterizes the great observers with a keen eye, the furrow of thinkers. The head was rather square-shape and her skin rather transparent to light. She had a small nose compared to mine, and she often reminded me of this. I had a big schnozz, she said. She had a wide mouth with an upper lip that was very thin with a nice curvature.

Her lower lip with an extraordinary mobility uncovered the many states of her mind, for she had a brilliant mind and a cunning memory. She often had a sad expression which translated her discontent with people and things, never with animals. Her very dark eyes had maintained the vivacity of youthfulness. The dark brown of her eyes contrasted with the light complexion while the silver of her hair gave her the air of a matriarch. Her hair was lightly curly and fell abundantly like silken strands down to her neck. She wore pants made of black velour and wore a long dark blue peasant blouse with fine embroidery on her shoulders, a garment that went down to her knees. I thought that was so extraordinary for a woman her age and of her reputation. Two magnificent buttons made of amethyst held her collar. There was an air of distinction and grace about her, and her venerable aspect then and there reminded me of the artistic scintillating touches of a Corot painting. That's how I saw her then and that's how I see her now in the higher spheres. Am I dreaming or not?

CHAPTER TEN

have shared with you so many things and experiences concerning Rosa Bonheur that I do not know what to do at this juncture. I suppose I could share the little indiscretions, as some people might say, but I leave that up to Rosa Bonheur. I am not one to start rumors or reveal things that belong in the obscure corners of the mind or of unfamiliar and rarely visited experiences. I am not made like that. I, Anna Klumpke, was the close and intimate friend of Rosa Bonheur and not her lover, as some people have intimated. There was certainly love between us but not sexual love or carnal attachment. That would have dishonored both Rosa Bonheur and me as independent, intelligent and creative women who sought artistry as a vocation in life. I know I have already said that before, but I needed to repeat it for I do not want any misunderstanding or lack of clear insight into my life with Rosa Bonheur. I feel so touched by my friend's love for me that I do not want that love to be diminished by false rumors and calumnies. Her life and my life as women and artists were dedicated to creative arts and nothing more. There were attractions to other people, I'm sure, on both our parts, but never was there any false and empty ones devoid of honesty and truth. I am not perfect and do not aspire toward perfection as a woman, but I do know that as a woman I am open and transparent, and I do not sell myself for the conspiracy of love affairs, women or men. I hate the term lesbian for it denounces the value of being a woman and a person. Let those who have those tendencies look upon them and consider that being out of the mold does not belittle them nor does it detract from the fact of being of one sex or another. Some people like to put tags on others, especially if one does not have what is considered by society, the normalcy of being a person, male and female. I am not a lesbian nor was I ever, and the same goes for Rosa Bonheur. Now, that's the end of that issue...I hope.

I have to make room for another person who will testify to Rosa Bonheur's talents and her art. So many things have been said about both, but there is still room for expansion. Rosa Bonheur's life and productivity as an artist demands that very little be left out if there is to be a transparency of time and history in the case of Rosa Bonheur. Nothing important is to be left out. After all, one's life cannot be measured only by spoonfuls but by pailfuls and pailfuls of evidence if not by a the only measure that is deemed necessary to bring out the outstanding features of one's life as it was lived. Rosa Bonheur's life was filled with marvelous deeds of self given to the expansion of art and personal aggrandizement in the field of what I would call *animalerie.* Please excuse my ranting here. If I were to expand on Rosa Bonheur's life and her work as an artist always in ebullition, I would have to say that her sphere of endeavors was so big that no one could ever measure it. I couldn't. It was always a new adventure after another one, never letting go of anything once achieved, and never forgetting the animal-like instinct that drove her to her beloved animals. She just could not avoid the link between her and animals that she considered soul-full. Yes, she even considered them to have a soul and a personality of their own. She felt connected to these qualities in all animals that she dealt with, and even those she never saw in person like those in the plains of Africa. A picture, a photo, a poster or even a lithograph brought that woman to her sense of discovery and artistry. She had to do a sketch first, sketch upon sketch, and follow up with a drawing and then, if it pleased her, a painting in oil. She never, as far as I know it, never jumped directly to the canvas for a work of art. She had to "practice" first, as she told me, practice until she got the full anticipated scheme of things with colors and textures down to the last detail, be it a single hair of a rabbit or a spot on a fawn grazing on the edge of the woods while his mother, the doe, looks after him. She had a keen eye, Rosa Bonheur, she did indeed, a very keen eye and a memory as sharp as a newly sharpened pencil. She remembered details upon details and stored them in her cache of memories so as to retrieve them when she needed to paint or draw something she was intent of reproducing with her sense of realism and never-ending delight. I called her a genius and she called me her apprentice genius. However, we both realized that we were far from being geniuses. It takes a long while, a very long while to experience enough and to master enough the full art of painting. Even with her "Horse Fair" painting, she always kept harping that there was something she should have or could have done to make it more complete and real. I told her that she had done her best and that people appreciated it to the extent that it was considered a masterpiece. "You want to know what a masterpiece is?" she would ask me. "A masterpiece is a work of art, of literature, of music, I must not forget music, of engineering, of architecture or whatever that demands intelligence and ripened skill to fully reproduce the genius behind the workings of the study done in solitude and perseverance." I simply used to nod my head in full agreement. "Furthermore, the word masterpiece is too often used to connote mediocrity and not excellence. *Un chef-d'oeuvre est une oeuvre transparente qui laisse entrevoir l'âme non seulement de l'artiste mais du sujet peint avec passion et détermination"* [it is a work that is transparent and allows insight into the soul of both artist and subject done with passion and determination]. *"Un chef-d'oeuvre n'est jamais, je le répète, jamais médiocre. Ce serait blasphémer l'idéal."* [A masterpiece is never, I repeat, never, mediocre. It would be like blaspheming the ideal]. Of course, I agreed with her for she was right all the time, as far as I was concerned. I was not a naive person and I did not take things lightly when it came to assess Rosa Bonheur's words and actions, but I did have my very own ideas and thoughts about certain things that Rosa Bonheur wasn't even aware of. I did not reveal all of my inner feelings and deeply ruminated thoughts to my friend. After all, I too had a private life and an intimacy that I wished to protect. Not that I hid things from her, but I simply did not reveal certain things that I wanted hidden. They were secret and secretly safe from others. After all, if I wanted to bare my soul in any fashion, I would have done it to the Creator who knows all things in all measures. At least, I was in the same mode of thinking as was Rosa Bonheur when it came to the Creator. We both were not religious persons, but neither were we anti-spiritual. We both believed in the Creator God and in the supremacy of the spirit that guides us into infinity. That's why Rosa Bonheur and I believed in the ultimate goal of life, that is, to die and meet again in the splendor of light and everlasting friendship that was meant to be. Rosa Bonheur always believed that she was to meet her mother some day as well as her dear Nathalie in the afterlife. That also included me. That is why she wanted me to be buried in the MICAS vault along with her remains and that of her dear, dear friend of long ago. I died in San Francisco and three years later my ashes were sent to Père Lachaise to be buried alongside of Rosa Bonheur, my friend in the arts and my dear friend in life and death. That may be sentimental for some but for Rosa Bonheur that was not just sentiment but soul-felt enlightenment on her part, and I shared that with her. Rosa Bonheur was neither an atheist nor an agnostic; she was a believer in the Divine Creator and the ultimate supremacy of the soul, as far as afterlife was concerned. She did not adhere to every dogma expounded by the Church nor did she follow every single ritual, but she respected them and she let others follow their own consciences when it came to religious convictions and beliefs. She was her own person, Rosa Bonheur. Woman, person and genuine human being made by the hands of the Creator to exemplify the great movements in nature and in the outerspheres. That is why she dedicated herself entirely to her art so that she might better exemplify what she saw with her own two eyes and what she believed in. That's commitment and a strong will at work. As far as I was concerned, there was no equal to Rosa Bonheur, only subscribers and followers. Yes, I place her on a pedestal of high regard and idealism. It does not take away her true sense of being human and achieving the very best as an artist, but it does mean that she was reaching for the stars as one fellow artist once told her, Eugène Delacroix.

Eugène Delacroix was an artist in the category of what was called Romanticism. Rosa Bonheur did not subscribe to Romanticism as a movement, but she did enjoy some of the works of artists such as, Delacroix, Géricault, and Ingres. She liked their vigor as artists, the life and extraordinary passion that they put into their work. For example, Delacroix's *Liberté Guidant le Peuple* [Liberty Guiding the People]. It's an extraordinary painting, full of patriotic vigor and daring boldness with the strength of a provocative work that shocked some. Some say that the young man or boy at the forefront is fashioned after Hugo's Gavroche of *Les Misérables*. Could be. That, I do not know, but it seems probable. It certainly stirs up the passions of some if not many. The daring boldness of the painter shows how much energy he poured into his work. The energy of a passionate artist at work. I'm not sure what defines Romanticism in the creative arts but I do know that the artistic endeavors of Romantic artists such as Delacroix are evidence of their commitment to color, movement, action, and especially passion. An artist must be passionate to paint such a work. Even the title or the theme hinges on the energy of passion. Who can really define or even paint *Liberté*. That's a provocative idea that the French truly admire and fight for. They have done it for centuries. Delacroix put on canvas this *idée maîtresse* that excites one's passion for freedom. Rosa Bonheur, as I have said, did not follow the tenets of artistic Romanticism but she did appreciate the work of some Romantic artists. She saw in some of their works the vital energy that stimulates creativity and puts one above the usual or habitual and even banal expressions of art and beauty. I'm getting to be overly pedantic or even idealistic about this artisitc movement and I should give way to artists who have, in the past, practiced their craft in a very creative way. I'm not sure if this is the time and place to do this, but I need to cede my words to another, in order to better define Rosa Bonheur's place in art history and give you readers an opportunity to not only meet such artists but enjoy what they have to say about art. You may ask what has this got to do with this particular novel. Well, it has a lot to do with it since we need to better understand the workings of an artist who was considered one of the best of her century. Rosa Bonheur had her influences and her ideas about artists that preceded her, after all, she did copy at the Louvre the works of so many of them that gave her the splendid opportunity not only to examine them closely but to fully appreciate their quality and artistic values. I must add that painters were not the only influence on her work and her ideas about art. There were the literary figures that she truly appreciated such as Cervantes, Sir Walter Scott, George Sand, Victor Hugo, Gustave Flaubert and several others. Words and ideas influence so many creators of art as do the artists who create on canvas, paper or any other medium. *Alors, je cède la parole à ces artistes, peintres et littérateurs.*

I am Ferdinand Eugène Victor Delacroix and I was relegated to the outer spheres which are reserved for artists of word and paintbrushes. If you ask me about music and its creators and composers, well, that's another category. Heaven was so enchanted with music and the entire range of creative artists that it created an entire sphere for them where angels who produce the heavenly music share this area of afterlife. Mozart is certainly one of them. So is Beethoven and one of Rosa Bonheur's favorite, Massenet. She loved his music and his operas such as "Manon". I love that opera and the romantic music that Massenet composed. I cannot help but to remember the Saint-Sulpice scene with Manon's aria *"Pardonnez-moi, Dieu de toute-puissance"* and the emotional pulsation that it sends right down to the bottom of the soles of your feet. At least, that's the way I sense it every time I hear it. Rosa Bonheur did not react to this aria as I did but she did tell me that her soul was deeply touched by the music and the words attached to it. One opera that really touched me and it did so very profoundly was Massenet's "Thaïs". Not just the story and the music in general but the inspirational and deeply touching music of the violin in the "Méditation" that everyone never fails to appreciate. It envelops you and brings you into the soul of meditation and deep thought while you try to relive every moment you had with your very own spirituality and contemplation of the ideal. Rosa Bonheur tried to recount to me what those moments were for her, but as hard as she tried she always broke down since many of those moments were related to her mother. Massenet's "Méditation" was for her the glimpse of the afterlife where her mother was waiting for her. Although she adored Mozart and his divine music, as she said, she placed Massenet's music right beside Mozart's, for she could not help being spiritually touched by strings being touched by an angel in "Méditation." Rosa Bonheur was not a romantic person but she certainly had strong vibrations of sentiments associated with Romaticism. After her pet lion, Fathma, died, I was told that Anna found her in her room quietly listening to Massenet's "Méditation". She did not dare interfere with this moment in her life because it was hers and hers alone. I realized then how much she loved and how attached she was to this animal, and why she had the passion to paint animals, and to believe in their vibrant personalities that she proclaimed as being real and vivid. That's how much she put such vigor and a sense of humanity into the animals she revered and painted. For me, it was simply incredible. I know of few artists who can appreciate the sensiblities of animals as she did. Well enough of music for now. It's not my category, not in my sphere, if you know what I mean. "Wait a minute,

Delacroix, It's my turn first. I preceded you in French painting. History and art history will attest to that."

My full name is Jean-Louis André Théodore Géricault. I'm a painter, a man of colors and textures, of perspective and light. I am especially known for paintings that represent epic adventures and historical depictions. I left the classroom choosing to study at the Louvre where, like Rosa Bonheur, I copied masterpieces: Rubens, Titian, Velazquez, and Rembrandt. I was good at it. I also spent a lot of time in Versailles where I found the stables of the palace. There I gained knowledge of the anatomy and movement of horses. Again, I was not unlike Rosa Bonheur who loved horses and put a lot of time and energy studying them. Her "Horse Fair" proves it. I was young and and I loved life. Some said that I was a handsome figure of a man. Some called me a dandy, a name that I did not refute.

As for my paintings, "The Charging Chasseur" that I called *Officier de chasseurs à cheval de la garde impériale changeant,* is one of my favorites. It depicts not only a horseman but a charger chasseur with his white steed on the battlefield. It is a dynamic, forceful and colorful representation, I must say. There's movement to it and no static stance as a painting. The officer is dressed in the finest of military uniform with an enormous hat with its jaunty red-tipped plume. I spent time painting the intricate horizontal braids, the tassels and the red belt. Such a fine figure of an *officier* in Napoleon's army. I painted this in a rented room in Paris in less than two weeks, so filled with enthusiasm and drive was I. I was very young then and I burned with the desire to become recognized in the art world. I chose a young *chasseur*, a military in retreat from Moscow. Napoleon's unquenchable imperial ambitions were under serious threat as never before. It's a huge painting of a lone man in the grips of terror, the terror of defeat. That's what I wanted to depict; that's what I wanted to paint. Not just the man but his horse. The horse is also under the threat of terror. We can see it in his bulging eyes. There is genuine fear there, and that's what I wanted to depict. The horse is not charging ahead but is retreating, and therefore we see his rump and his flowing white tail in the foreground. It's a caparisoned horse with a leopard-skin pelt where sits the officer. I even put in the head of the leopard to render it more exotic and daring. Some called this my romantic inclination at work. The young man has a red-blondish mustache and was well-known in Paris. Unfortunately, he died in battle. This painting received critical acclaim when it was first exhibited. It even stirred strong emotions on the part of people who sensed a loss and a terrible blow to the Napoleonic empire. It was all a glorious self-deception on the part of Napoleon who wanted to be the great leader and emperor of the civilized world. I always doubted that he would reach his goal. He was a great mastermind, the little corporal who had visions of greatness.

I cannot depart without saying a word about my great painting that critics called a masterpiece, "The Raft of the Medusa", *Le Radeau de la Méduse.* Everyone talked about it, some praising it, others damning it for its macabre realism. It was real. After all, it was based on a contemporary French shipwreck whereby the captain abandoned his ship and let the crew and passengers die in the troubled waters. The incident became a national scandal . It was truly an indictment of the corrupt establishment. "I posed for one of the figures in this painting, do you remember?" "Yes, Delacroix, you did." "We were good friends then and I learned a lot from you. I wish you had not died so young. *Mon Dieu, trente-deux ans!*" "Yes, *mon ami,* I got chronic tubucular infection and that took me away, my life and my career as an artist who would have continued *d'épater le monde de l'art.*" Stun the art world. I truly believed that. "Wait a minute there. You were no Rubens and no Rembrandt. Just a young painter who turned heads around just to glimpse at what was called Romanticism in art." "I was not a Romantic. I was an artist dedicated to color, movement and epic events in history." "How about the paintings of insane persons?" "That's something else. I'm glad that I did that. They were real persons with real causes of insanity." My end came soon enough, too soon. And, like Rosa Bonheur I was buried at Père Lachaise among the immortals.

"My turn now, Géricault. You've talked long enough. You have to give a chance to others to express themselves while, we artists, have an opportunity to do so in the great novel that is being woven for Rosa Bonheur the woman and her splendid works." "Great? Great novel? That's not what a Shakespeare, a Cervantes or a Flaubert would say, I'm sure. Our writer is a mediocre, if not inconsequential author. Too bad we don't have someone else, someone with a certain fame and exuberance to write our story." "It's not our story, Géricault. It's Rosa Bonheur's. This is, after all, a literary vehicle in the hands of a published author who is doing his best to write Rosa Bonheur's story, and he's spending a lot of time doing it. He spent much effort and time to find the right angle to his novel, and he believes he has found it by letting the main characters speak beyond the grave, and that includes us. We do not have too often the chance to talk about ourselves and our work beyond the grave. Others do it for us, but we ourselves do not. This is a wondrous privilege for me." "I'm grateful as an artist, but I would have liked someone more spectacular in the literary arts." "You're the youthful one, inexperienced in life and maturity, romantic." "Let me get on with my story will you."

My name is, but I've already told you my name. Delacroix. I am one of the leaders of the French Romantic school and I'm not ashamed of it. I know that Rosa Bonheur was not too inclined to appreciate Romanticism in the arts but she did acquire the knowledge and taste of some works such as my *Liberté guidant le peuple*. I know this was a very patriotic work and filled with romantic passion, but I just had to do it. It was in my guts. A lot of people loved it while some others thought it was too romantic and too gory. I did it because I wanted to and express my feelings about what the French are so adamant about, LIBERTÉ. What would we do without it and what would happen to our country if we did not have freedom, freedom of expression, freedom of activities, freedom of speech and freedom to create as we artists do. That's why Rosa Bonheur liked this painting because she recognized the great value of freedom. She was indeed a free spirit that one.

I also created other works such as "Royal Tiger" where you see a large tiger crouching, ready to pounce, the eyes glaring and the nose smelling the prey. This lithograph was really inspired by a tiger that I saw in the Paris zoo since I did not go in the wild to search for wild animals, and I certainly did not have animals in my home like Rosa Bonheur did. I did have a great empathy for the natural world and was fascinated by animals. All you have to do is look at my paintings of Arab horses and my lion hunt. Animals have a life of their own, and Rosa Bonheur certainly captured that distinctive life. *Chapeau!* All in all, I tended to explore color and movement rather than the clarity of lines as Ingres did. "Now, let's not have Ingres in this conversation for we'll never finish it. He's so precise and determinedly proud that one cannot get in a word edgewise." "Yes, Géricault, let's not get too involved here. After all, we're allowed to come out of the sphere to talk about Rosa Bonheur, and not the entire panoply of French artists.

However, let's make way for the great one, the academic one, the one who followed the rules of the game."

"Now is my turn and do not make fun of me and my work." My name is Jean-Léon Gérôme. It is true that I am an academician as an artist and teacher. I not only painted but taught many students in the process of exercizing my craft. I truly enjoyed sharing my artistic experience with students who were serious about painting and intelligent enough to ask questions of me. I do not like dumb students who do not dare to open their mouths. I know, I know that some teachers prefer not to have students questioning them, but I do, and I always enjoyed explaining things to talented students.

Well, I must tell you, at the beginning of my career as an artist, I was terribly disappointed when I failed to obtain the prestigious Prix de Rome since they told me that my figure drawing was inadequate. That was a lesson for me, and I tried that much harder to perfect my drawing skills. Back in Paris, I joined the *Boîte de Thé,* a group of studios in the Rue Notre-Dame-des-Champs that became a meeting place for artists, writers and actors. George Sand entertained in the small theater of a studio. I thought she had great talent as a performer and as a writer. I know that Rosa Bonheur admired her. I also know that my paintings had Classical subjects and I enjoyed doing them. People admired many of my paintings. I was a regular guest of Empress Eugénie at the Imperial Court of Compiègne. I'm so very glad that the Empress recognized and rewared Rosa Bonheur for her excellent work. Now for my masterwork that I called *L'Éminence Grise.* It's a depiction of the main stair hall of the palace of Cardinal Richelieu.That was my main perspective and focus. I saw the geometrical grandeur of the stairway while the friar is descending slowly while reading the Bible. He pays no attention to the people on his right who either bow to him or gaze at him. Power draws power and people bow to it or even grovel in front of it as we see here. I believe I captured very well François LeClerc du Trembly, a Capuchin friar known as the Grey Eminence then, as he is descending the ceremonial staircase. Rosa Bonheur once told me that she liked that depiction and especially the staircase for it rendered the painting a majestic sense, although she never liked classical or academic paintings, as such, but she did admire some of them for their mastery and strong and deliberate colors. She remembered seeing some at the Louvre while she was copying the masters. She also told me that she liked my painting "On the Desert" with the two dogs and the Arab with a leash. It was the atmosphere, the muted sense of the desert that she liked, she said, although she also liked the two dogs. She regretted not having the chance to visit the great deserts of the world like the Sahara and the Gobi. I told her never to give up for all possibilities are there for one who creates and paints. She thanked me and went away uplifted for I know she was on her way to greatness. I must now pass you to one of Rosa Bonheur's colleagues, the much acclaimed painter, Bouguereau.

My name is William-Adolphe Bouguereau. My family recognized early on that I had talent for drawing and painting, especially my unle, the priest. Eventually, I attended l'École des Beaux Arts in Paris where I excelled in my studies. I even attended animal dissections and learned about the precisions of bones, ligaments and muscles. That's one thing that Rosa Bonheur did in her slaughterhouse days and got to know very well. My works appeared annually at the Paris Salon where I first met Rosa Bonheur. At first, she seemed to be a bit indifferent about my paintings, but with time, some of them grew on her, especially those of little girls. I'll talk more about that later.

Speaking of the Paris Salons, one reviewer stated that I had a natural instinct and knowledge of contour, and that the *eurythmie* of the human body preoccupied me. He was right, of course The human body, especially the human female body, not only preoccupied me but fascinated me. Raphael was my master, my very admired and favorite painter. I loved his artistic touch and the shimmering glow that he brought to his paintings. People in the know said that I had a photo-realistic style that brought to life goddesses, bathers, shepherdesses, and madonnas. They were right, of course. That's what I intended to do with my experience as a painter, to follow line, contour and expressible sensual tones and beauty. I used my influence to open many French art institutions to women for the first time for which Rosa Bonheur was ever grateful. She wanted so much to open all venues to women be they art, scientific techniques, or any other expression of talent and skill. I loved my studio and could not wait to get back to it in the morning. That's where I thrived as a man of creativity. That's what gave me the enthusiasm for art as art should be, an expression of fidelity to nature and human nature. The Impressionist avant-garde and

Degas reviled me as an artist, and made fun of me and my work, "slick and artificial surfaces," they called it. They simply did not understand my work nor did they appreciate the creativity that went into it. Some even said that I painted for money. Well, I did in a way but don't artists paint to make a living as well as expressing themselves creatively?

Coming back to the three canvasses that Rosa Bonheur liked, there's the "Daisies" *"La Frileuse"*, and "Fishing for frogs." She liked *"Daisies"* not simply for the little girl dressed in blue with the quiet girlish eyes, the heart-shaped red lips, and her pale complexion. The small daisies on the stone bench with a single daisy in her right hand are the brightness that daisies bring to an open field where most probably the little girl picked them. There is a sense of whiteness and purity in nature that daisies bring to life, and that's what I wanted to bring to this painting. The little girl is an important feature of this work, but I also think that the daisies bring freshness to it and heighten the naturalness of it all. As for *"La Frileuse"* a word difficult to translate in English meaning very sensitive to cold. This is a painting of a young girl with the soft pearl-like skin sheen of face and bare arms and shoulders, especially the completely uncovered right shoulder. It's no wonder she's cold, but I had to reveal her splendid skin tone. Her full head of auburn hair, her left ear with a drop gold earring with a red stone at he top, her demure smile and shiny nose as well as her sleek eyebrows give her that resplendency that I admire and paint with a certain voluptuousness even in a young girl. However, it's her eyes that conjure up a certain female look that is both sensually alluring and at the same time innocently captivating. She seems to be cold but shows srong feminine warmth. She's altogether at the crossroads of tender age with budding, femininity. She is Raphael's tender *femme-en-beauté-naturelle,*

As for "Fishing for frogs" this is a canvas that draws our attention to two young girls sitting on the stone embankment of a pond. One has a pole and the other simply looks at her. There is a reflection of tender innocence here. The little girl holding the short pole is looking downward not paying any atttention to her friend. She seems to be in a daydreaming faze, looking serious while casting for frogs. She has her left arm around the other little girl's shoulders. I wanted to depict them as good friends. The other little girl is looking directly into her friend's face. She is wearing a sweet smile while gazing at her friend. There is total innocence here, the innocence of youth and intimacy with nature. That's what Rosa Bonheur liked about this work, the naturalness of sujects and nature. The background is somber wooded dark green leaves. Both little girls are barefooted. The skin tones are bright and youthful, fresh as springtime in nature. The simplicity in this painting is also a characteristic that emanates from the subject matter and the colors as well as the texture of the clean and precise brushstrokes. That's what I like about my paintings. They represent the finest of my experiences as an artist seeking beauty and delight in his work. Nothing else. Now, I am told that it's time for the artists of literature, for they are artists in their own right. At least, that's the way I see them. Ah, literarure the art of putting words together and making them sing with brightness and thought-provoking melodies. But, it's not for me to describe literature best, although I'm a lover of books and stories well defined and well put together. "Stop talking Bouguereau. Leave the stage for others." "Oui, Monsieur Géricault." You readers are off to another sphere, the sphere of literature, especially the literature that Rosa Bonheur liked and kept reading.

CHAPTER ELEVEN

My name is Miguel de Cervantes Saavedra. I was a soldier, novelist, poet, playwright and accountant. Yes, accountant. I had to earn a living at one time. I am in this sphere on account of my being a novelist. I am in very good company as you will see. I am especially known for my novel *Don Quixote* and without bragging too much, as the greatest writer in the Spanish language with my novel considered to be the first modern novel. That's quite something in the literary world. I would dare say in the entire world of creativity. My influence on the Spanish language is such that it is often called *la lengua de Cervantes,* the language of Cervantes. How's that for a lasting influence. I wasn't always a writer, although I had a great *inclinaciòn* for writing. I even went to jail for discrepancies in my accounts. That was not a period of my life that I enjoyed.

When I undertook *Don Quixote,* I decided to write the novel in parts. And when the first part came out and found immediate success, well, I knew I had found my *nicho* in life. I settled in Madrid and decided to devote the rest of my life to writing. The reason I'm here with you is that Rosa Bonheur thought my novel was simply great and so entertaining that she adopted it as her favorite reading and read it over and over again. She had good taste, I must say. Most of Rosa Bonheur's friends knew of her fondness for my novel. She had a love for old romances and of chivalry. She spoke of the novel quite often to a point that she even recalled certain adventures of this story and dwelt on the hero, Don Quixote, with all of his adventures with which she was well acquainted. Among others, there was Don Quixote tilting against the windmills. Yes, I must say that my novel truly fascinated her. I guess that the adventure of the windmills truly fascinated her, and so many others who have determined that this chivalric adventure of a madman gone wild has resonated profoundly in their minds and their imagination enough to make it an icon of sorts. Why, there are so many sculptures of this man, Don Quixote, the man from La Mancha, artistically made as a work of art or fabricated as an unworthy and cheap souvenir, either plastic, cardboard, brass, or wood. I don't like them, but trourists and souvenir collectors like them. Overall, I'm glad that people think so highly of my imaginary hero who goes mad reading romances days on end, and even in the dark of night. He has become truly an icon of the imagination at work gone wild and crazy enough to imagine monsters, windmills that fly in the wind, ladies in distress and ladies that elicit chivalric love for a knight-errant on the move. All of the episodes or adventures in "Don Quixote" are based on my experiences with people, their senseless behavior, and their way of acting and thinking, as well as the readings of certain authors who conjured up the romances that stirred the imagination of all those readers who let themselves be enslaved by imagined adventures of knights and ladies of old.

Rosa Bonheur was not only an *animalière* but a reader of classics and other writings because she had a fine mind for reading. She knew that being an artist is not just painting and sketching, but filling one's mind and imagination with thoughts, colorful and inspiring thoughts that develop into creative outbursts of the soul. It is out of the soul that bursts the creative processes and gives the artist and writer, as well as the composer, the creativity to imagine and create works of art either on canvas, on paper or on a music script. I have experienced such processes and developed in the silence of my working table at night and sometime in the early hours of the morning the energy to write and experience the splendid joy of writing. Word after word came to me, and as I put them on paper. I could visualize the power of writing and the magic of thoughts on paper. I also realized that I coud make people think, laugh, smile and shed tears of either gladness or sorrow. I had them in the palm of my hands and I was able to influence their mode of thought and share the delight of communication with words. I had the power to sway opinion, mold commitments, carve out deep essential thoughts, and entertain while using irony, subtle mockery, purposeful satire while inferring revelations of human weaknesses, and above all open the eyes of those whose eyes needed to be open to truth. All I had to do was to look at people, really look at them, scrutinize and analyze their actions and motives as they wandered in their daily lives. It is so easy to get to learn about people and even systems when you put your mind to it. It is the *condicìon humana* that is displayed before your very eyes, and all you have to do as a writer is to divulge it in the creative mode of expressing things. That is the art of writing, as far as I'm concerned.

Well, enough of deliberations on writing. I'm going to give you some facts about myself so that you may better understand me and my writing, specifically *Don Quixote* the novel so admired by Rosa Bonheur. *Don Quixote* was not my first writing but my most important one. It took a long time for it to emerge from my pen after I had spent days, months and even years dwelling on the subject matter and the words I was going to use after my deliberations. A novel does not simply sprout out of one's head like the Greek goddess, Athena, but it takes much thinking and sifting through experiences both literary and personal to make a novel emerge from one's mind and imagination. Yes, it takes imagination, creative imagination to spin a novel. How is one to create if one does not rely on the imaginative processes with which we human beings are endowed. Some never make use of their imagination. They think it's fake and unreal. It produces nothing but lies and fabrications. They're simply dogs or puppets. Even dogs have some kind of imagination. Some people do not see. I mean they do not realize that they do not grasp the intensity of the moment and the magic of responding to it in a way so as to create some form of clear and precise expression of the imagination at work. Here I go again, making comments on the art of writing. That's because I need to express my views on it and impart them to those who need to reflect on them. Otherwise, I would miss my opportunity to educate my readers and possible followers even from this otherworldly sphere. I am making the most of this opportunity given to me while I can and while my time here to express myself is short and fleeting.

Don Quixote was a man of letters. By this, I mean he loved to read. He had entire shelves of books, shelves beyond shelves of books, and books stored in boxes in his attic. He never gave away any books nor did he get rid of any of them. It's only the priest and the barber who encouraged and even incited the housekeeper to throw the books outside in the yard and then burn them because they thought that the books were at the very origin of his madness and folly. Don Quixote loved to read, daylight, early in the morning, afternoons and evenings late into the night sometimes. Quite often he forgot to eat. His food was the written stories that appealed to him as nourishment. He grew skinnier and skinnier. He would sit there and read hours and hours at a time forgetting that he had chores to do and responsibilities to accomplish. But he did not care. His entire life was poured into books, especially when he discovered the romances, I mean the medieval stories of courtly love. There he found solace to his life, lean and meager from being denied the human love of a woman. The passionate and burning love of a woman that would sear his heart and rivet his soul to the passion of love. He found that in his books he could reach the stars and even the moon, if he so desired. That became his great challenge in life. He admired the way the writers such as Chrétien de Troyes accomplished this. Courtly love, knights on horseback, damsels in a faraway castle pining for their knights wanderers, and the burning thoughts of finally meeting the love of their life, all that was part of the adventures of courtly adventures of yore. If one lets books claim his entire life, as it did with Don Quixote, then he becomes obsessed with them and their contents to a point that they become illusions. Illusions that spark illusionary actions such as the wandering knight in search of love and adventure as seen in the great exploit and adventure, or I should say folly, of Don Quixote that shaped his entire existence once bitten by the bug of romantic adventures. Once these adventures become real in the mind of a Don Quixote, they become the spirit that spurs on not only the mind but also the body into realizing what the imagination had wrought. It is the imagination gone wild. Courtly love romances then become the pattern with which the mind guides itself and plunges into the opportunity of new adventures unfolding before your very eyes. Reality takes a back seat and imaginary scenes unfold as time unfolds, and even people you encounter along the way become part of the imaginary adventure. You have now created your own imaginary world and that's what Don Quixote did, poor fellow. Inns become castles, windmills as flying monsters, clouds of dust raised by flocks of sheep interpreted as two armies coming together to do battle on the plains, and the monstrous wineskins attacked by the sword of a zealous mad knight, and more. The adventures of Don Quixote are real in that sense, splendid in their allurement and fulfilling in their intensity to fill one's heart and soul with woeful delight. The illusion of things being real is an illusion that cannot be changed unless reality sets in and banishes what is imagined as real, but that is hard to do since the illusion created is very real to the one who imagines things. It is an endless pursuit of what is conceived as reality turned into what is illusory. That is what I created with this novel of a poor soul out to seek the awesome advenure of his life, a life that had laid lifeless and soulless for years before it took on the life of a knight wanderer. My main character and my plot for the novel is really based on the dangers of letting your imagination ride with the wild wind of illusions. It also gave me the creative opportunity to smile and even laugh at myself and others who create for themselves the burden of the heart and soul gone awry. I contemplated the actions and words of people who did just that, and added to it the possibilities of estrangement from the reality of everyday living. That's all.

"Is that all, friend of writers?" "Who said that?" "*C'est moi, Flaubert.*" "Ah, Flaubert, the writer who consumes my soul by writing about a woman who is also mystified and taken over by romances. There are similarities between Don Quixote and Madame Bovary, as careful readers have noticed....Chrétien de Troyes, Cervantes and Flaubert are the links, some say, to the illusion of love and imaginary adventures. Why, I have heard that Madame Bovary is the female Don Quixote, is that true?" "I have read your novel, an excellent creative accomplishment of writing. I do not know if my creation of a woman who loses sight of reality has similar views and dreams as Don Quixote's." "They're both highhly influenced by romances." "I know but are they cut from the same cloth?" "One is a man and the other a woman." "I know that. You don't have to stress the obvious." "All I have to say right now Signor Flaubert is that I'm going to steal your thunder before you speak. " "What thunder?" "*Disculpo, Signor Flaubert but I must say, Soy yo* Don Quixote." "Oh, you mean '*Madame Bovary, c'est moi*'" "*Si, oui.*" How's that possible since you have never said that of Don Quixote before?" "Well, I now realize that much of what I have Don Quixote say and do is predicated on me and my life experiences as a man and writer. You see I did not only write but I read a lot, and sometimes

I let all of that seep into my soul and convert me from a reader to one who imagines things seriously. We are all Don Quixote to an extent, are we not? " "Are we all Madame Bovary to some extent?" "That's a real question to be pondered." "By the way I never said *Madame Bovary, c'est moi*."

You see, dear reader and listener, I chose to satirize the chivalric romance so that I might uncover the madness of many readers who took these romances as reality and led unfruitful lives if not of desperation at least of frustration and, at times, gloom. The writing allowed me, Cervantes, to illuminate various aspects of human nature and the fragility of human weaknesses. We are all cast from the same mold but we do not all have the same predestination. Some have reasonable goals and perspectives while others dance to the tune of self-delusions. We are all on the border of sanity and insanity. We can so easily fall into the cracks. You see, Don Quixote is a great admirer of everything that is good and great blended with a relative kind of madness. I was often asked what made the guy tick. I answered that my pen did. By that, I meant that what I wrote was what I considered to be the product of an imagination at work after having studied the inclinations, quirks, foibles and strengths of the human being in a given society, but also reflected, in a sense, in the entire human race, for we are all from the same root, the same genus.

I paired Don Quixote with a character of opposite qualities, Pancho Sanza. I do not have enough time to elaborate on him. But, Pancho is composed of grossness and simplicity, a simplicity of innocence and awe faced with the wonder of new adventures and the promise of the throne of Denmark or a governorship somewhere. He needs a knight who chases windmills to open him up to things that bring wonderment, but a wonderment of simplicity and innocence. I cannot imagine Don Quixote without Sancho Panza for it would be like taking the reflection of reality from his life and his adventures as a self-proclaimed knight out to meet and probably resolve the challlenges of the world, a world filled with imaginary possibilities. One is overly educated while the other is not educated. One is committed to over indulgence in reading while the other can hardly read at all. He cannot write either. He is totally uneducated. His mind is a blank on which nothing of importance has ever been written. As I have said before, "*Quien anda mucho y lee mucho, sabe mucho y ve mucho*...who walks much and reads much, knows and sees much. That's all I have to say, for that 's all that's is allotted me. By the way, I wish to thank Gustave Doré for his magnificent illustrations of my novel, "Don Quixote." I really like the one showing Don Quixote sitting on an old wing chair reading out loud, raising high his sword in his right hand and exclaiming his ambitious dream to go on the ever challenging quest of the knight in armor, as he sits surrounded by visions of his fantasy. I admire this illustration and the one showing Don Quixote tilting with the windmills. What marvelous talent and what great skill of illustration on the part of Monsieur Doré.

I must say before I leave that Rosa Bonheur liked my novel because it made her smile and kept her entertained in her life as an artist. She knew that art requires nourishment and reading added to the quench of hunger and thirst of the mind and soul. Besides, she must have felt the need to pursue her imagination and vitality of creativity when she was growing up by reading stories that validated her pursuits as a person who wanted so much to remain true to herself as a woman. Living needs both the truth of reality and the truth of the imagination.*"Vamos a ir, Flaubert, es su turno.* "Your turn."

*Et bien, oui, c'est mon tour de parler de l'écriture...*my turn to talk about writing. "Before the two of you go their separate ways, I have to insert my views on literature and writing."

I am Chrétien de Troyes, readers, and I have something to say too. After all, you Cervantes and Flaubert, you both realize that you blamed me and my romances in a way as to disparage me and my writings. That my writings influenced a Don Quixote and a Madame Bovary in a deleterious way. You scorned me and blamed me for the ills of your times. All I did was to entertain the ladies at court of my times, Eleanor of Aquitaine and her daughter, Marie of France, Countess of Champagne. It was a purposeful task mine was. As a *trouvère* I did what was expected of me and I did it well. I alleviated the boredom of uselessness and empty hours at court. I filled the hours of the the elite class of women who had nothing else to do but dream of adventures, especially the adventures of the quest of love. You both know that love had ever been a quest of some kind, fulfilled or unfulfilled, realized or not realized. It still is today on earth, poor souls who cannot get it right about love. Many are the humans who crave for it but cannot truly find it. They are forever on the quest for the fulfillment of love but they will never reach their goal. Love is unattainable if one searches in the realm of entertainment and party-going. *L'ennui est incontrôlable car il ne peut pas s'écarter de la fabrication d'un coeur si souvent mal à l'aise...* Ennui, and there is no other real translation for it, is incontrolable for it cannot be cast aside from the fabrications of a heart so very often ill at ease. Ennui serves no purpose other than darken the soul and lead it astray from its very purpose in life. Only true love can assuage the heart and soul. And so, you see, I served a purpose at a time when purposelessness reigned at court. The knights that I invented for my romances were the epitome of *la largesse d'âme et de coeur*...the generosity of the soul and the heart. That was found in the knight who played out this quality of being and, I may add, acting out his purpose at court. Women were placed on the proverbial pedestal then and venerated like madonnas. Some liked it while others desired a more sensual approach to their daily lives. I fulfilled their adventures of the heart in a way that was acceptable at court. Courtly love had to conform with courtly rules of living and behaving. I'm sorry if some people took all of this too seriously and did not understand my writings to be of the imagination, a bridled imagination and not an unbridled one. Senor Cervantes I speak for all the romance writers especially the author of "Amadis of Gaul" Garci Ordonez de Montalvo. Also and especially of Feliciano de Silva and his romances that you mention in your great novel. You said that you did not like his bombastic style and his extravagant tales, and so you decided to satirize him and his works. I know that he did not exactly please some people with his romances but he was and still is in the tradition of storytellers, good or bad. Cervantes you and Flaubert you too used me and my writing so that you two might gain favor with your reading public in a way to disparage me and my romances. Did you have a social role in mind? Did you think that reading romances could easily influence the hearts and minds of human beings? Only if they were disposed to irrationality and illusions, I would say. So both of you invented characters that were prone to madness. The madness of a misdirected imagination, and you gave the world by so doing an insight into its own weaknesses and madness. Isn't that right? You blame me for the madness of people who cannot control their sanity. You have planted them in a world of wild imaginary possibilities brought about by a lack of rational and sane realisation of things and even themselves. But that 's alright, my fame has remained unstinted throughout the ages. " "I, Flaubert, did not mean to disparage you and your writing. I only inferred that romances put to an extreme of abused imaginary states can corrupt the reality of things and put to shame the order of living in a well-balanced world of thoughts and sentiments. That's all." "You, Flaubert, are a nerd as they say in today's parlance. You overstate everything and try to philosophize your way out of things. Bah!" "Aurevoir, fellow writers, I need not stay with you while you wrangle about things especially writing." "*Adios,* Chrétien de Troyes, great teacher and man of letters who influenced so many writers throughout the ages."

I'm now taking over since it's my time and I will take what is allotted to me. I am Gustave Flaubert and I am a recognized writer. Writing as art, I must say. Not all writings are artistic in their form and content. Writing is an arduous task and one has to experience the hardship of writing before accomplishing anything worthwhile. That takes time and energy. How to get started in all of this is the big question.We are not born with it and neither do we attain the level of talent for writing when we are young. Good writing comes with maturity. And, I also believe that the measure of good writing is in the measure of passion. Mediocrity is far from passion and I must say it is the bane of simpletons like Charles Bovary. Between Madame Bovary, Charles and the rest of them is a fellow that I name Homais. Homais is the antithesis of Madame Bovary, but one who soothes the political and societal warped consciences of a bourgeois class that is too centered on its rise to popularity and the chase after medals awarded ever so often to unmeritorious individuals. Fools. Homais is the ultimate fool who believes that science will redeem him from his mediocrity and advance him in the thwarted sight of those in power, the power of the intelligentia. Homais cowtows to anyone who will bring him recognition. He's a sham, a hypocrite and a man who is filled with the illusion of self-aggrandizement.

On the other hand, there is Rodolphe who counts on his manhood to build up and deploy his passion for the little woman such as Emma Bovary of seemingly weak character and gullible for the adventure of love, but his is a waning self-destructive passion. Rodolphe is the center of his own being, a man devoured by his own self-importance and gritty pride that gnaws at his passion of being a man. There is also passion in Léon but it's a childish and immature one not ready for self-deployment into the world of reality. Léon is mama's boy and he will not tear himself away from her apronstrings until they are broken by her. Léon is a child gone astray from the real passion of love. It's a non-passion passion. An inclination towards the passion of love that never comes to full fruition.

Emma Bovary is led to her illusions by way of self-immolation on the ardent embers of what she thinks is love and the adventures of love predicated on so much reading that causes her to imagine love as in a book of chivalric adventures. The many pious readings of the convent stimulate her heart and its desires to fly over the nets of self-destruction by means of sacrifices and penance. She is also an ambitious woman, one who can do or die for anything that becomes her goal and soothes her passion. She is caught in the dilemma of wanting to live life to its fullest and the appreciation of what reality brings to her everyday life. She cannot stand mediocrity and wants everything that will erase the dumbness and lackluster of mediocrity as personalized by her husband, Charles. It's so dull to be mediocre without the stimulus of passion. *Joie de vivre* is her motto. We all have that same motto engraved into our hearts, but we do not all push it to extremes. I never said that *Madame Bovary, c'est moi* but I could have said it only because I realized that I harbored some of the same tendencies and weaknesses that hounded her. I was often led by my passions in love, lust and, of course, my dermination to write, write well and without relying on a style of writing that was old and treacherous, *déchu*. I put in so much time and energy developing my own style, and I'm very proud of what I did. I sought exactitude and preciseness. Furthermore, I accomplished what I set out to do, transform my sense of Romanticism into a commitment to realism. Emma Bovary dies at the end because she cannot face the horrible truth that she has failed, and no one will accept her as the woman she is or turned out to be. She has nothing more to give a man. She has no more financial resources and is crushed under the terrible burden of debts. She can no longer buy her way out. *Elle est déchue...*she is a fallen woman. She can no longer claim the social and married name of Madame Bovary. It's tarnished and lackluster. There is only one way out, suicide, the snuffing out of a life that led to perdition and now condemns her to mediocrity and even less than that, poverty and wretchedness. That is her greatest fear. A return to nothingness, the nothingness of being alone and without the stimulus of passion. *C'est la passion inassouvie et délavée comme un torchon qui l'énerve à n'en mourir* ...it's passion unquenched and washed-out like an old rag that rattles her nerves enough to die from it. I wanted to show what happens to a woman who lets herself be driven by romantic delusions and falters when she learns that nothing works anymore, not even her passion for living and loving. Even her death by arsenic is a terrible *ennui* for her. I could elaborate here on the great romantic *ennui, ce mal du siècle,* but it's not time to undertake this right now. I have other things I want to mention. "Hurry, Flaubert because my turn has been skipped." "I know, Sir Walter Scott, but allow me to finish, then you can take step on the pedestal of the writer that you are. That's where your readers have put you and you have given them romantic stories to assuage their longing for love and adventure, the English way. " " Oh, stop ranting and let's him procede with his story." "Why do you always think that I'm belligerent and wacky? Why are you ever on my case, as they say in the contemporary world, Spanish man and writer?" "Oh, shut up. You're a great fart in the world of letters. That's all I have to say, you French *friandise séchée...dulce duro.* You have lost all *sabor.*" "I will ignore that coming from the mouth of one who decries the true flavor and taste of letters." "Watch out, for the world of readers and critics say just the opposite and they are mystified by my writing. They know what true literature is." " I stand in awe of your accomplishments, Master of satire and of rightful indulgence in the *mot juste.* " "Thank you. You did just that my fellow writer. The *mot juste, la palabra justa,* was your contribution to the art of the French novel." "Why, thank you for noticing my strength and contribution to good writing, Cervantes." "Let's stop complimenting one another. Time is fleeting when one is given it, although time does not exist here on this sphere."

As I was saying, I have other things I wanted to mention while it's my turn to speak. I never let any circumstances rob me of the determination to speak out especially when it comes to writing. "Hurry on, Monsieur Flaubert." "*Oui, Maître des grandes histoires d'amour et d'aventures.* He thinks he can shame me with his royal title and his Edinburough style of parlance, but I'll show him that *un Français peut tout aussi bien parler avec droiture et perspicacité qu'une tête de bois franc...*a Frenchman can speak with righteousness and perspicacity as well as a hardheaded bloak. " "I heard that, Flaubert of the sick-in-the-head Bovary." Enough you guys, the sphere is getting to be a sphere of quarrels and name-calling...*ça suffit.*

Well, what I wanted to say is this. Though my novel "Madame Bovary" is my delight as a writer, and I recognize it, as so many people do, to be a masterpiece, I must confess that my very favorite piece of writing is the tale, "The Simple Heart"....*Un coeur simple.* I had to say it in French because it means so much more to me; it touches the romantic fibers of my heart although I hate to admit this. You see, all my life I fought the bourgeois tendencies of my people and I tried to overcome them with satire and a sense of obfuscation. With time, I came to despise those of *mon entourage héréditaire et culturel...*my hereditary and cultural sourroundings that was Rouen and its surrounding towns and villages. Paris attracted me and fascinated me with its grandeur and rich history of striking historical people that formed the very fiber of this city. But, I just could not deny and extricate from myself the province where I was born and lived for so many years. It was like a bloodsucker stuck on my flesh never to be removed. I had to live with it and do my best to turn it into an art form that without extricating it would be metamorphosized into the butterfly reflex. I would turn the ugliness of my plight to the beauty of art and writing. That's what I accomplished with "Madame Bovary" and especially "Un coeur simple." I love the woman called Félicité, the woman of the simple heart who manages to overcome a sad and penniless childhood and emerge as a loving person, first with Théodore, then Paul and Virginie followed by the nephew, Victor. She even loves Madame Aubain in her own way of dispelling the onery disposition of the mistress. Unlike Emma Bovary, Félicité is a loving and giving person who is far from attaching herself to the luxuries of life. She is simple in her tastes, in her heart and simple in her soul. It is true that she can easily be swayed by religious fervor and the liturgical movements and displays, but Félicité remains herself, the simple woman of the provincial countryside. She never aspired to be great nor noticed by the good bourgeoisie that set her aside simply as a maid and cook. I love Félicité but at the same time I abhor her. I mean that I cannot subscribe to her simplemindedness and her peasant ways of thinking and doing things. But I do love her genuine soul and her lack of frightful pride. She has a transparent soul and loving heart. Félicité loses everyone she loves and at the end, she even loses her favorite being in the world, this animal called, Loulou, the parrot. I do not think that Félicité's story is sentimental and especially not mawkish, but rather a story of a poor soul who finds the mystical outlet of her existence. At the end of her misery here on earth, she sees a gigantic parrot filled with light in the midst of the wafts of incense that appease the sensuality of her nostrils and her sense of smell. She swoons into the spirit of light and fervor. We are all sensual as human beings, and so is Félicité of the simple heart. I kept the realism of the story while injecting a sense of mysticism into it although I know that some people will chide me for saying this. I knew what I was doing. A writer has the freedom to do as he sees fit according to his norms of writing in the pursuit of the *mot juste.* There is much more that I could say, but my time is up and I must cede the platform to Sir Scott. Yes, it's a lovley platform where silence and peace reign without the interferences of earthly daily life. I wonder if I will ever write again...

Enough, Flaubert, enough. It's good to hear about established and renowned writers, but one can just hear so much about their devices for writing, their stylistic norms, their tendencies to elaborate on their subject matter, and above all, their self-proclaimed importance to the literary world. Let me get away from all of this chattering about writing. I have no literary norms as far as the actual writing goes, at least, no claims to the perfect poem or novel. I just wrote, that is all. Whatever came to me and my talent for writing is what I produced as literature. At least what people call literature. I do not believe in mediocrity either, Flaubert, but I do believe in the perfection of words and ideas and that takes time and energy of the mind as well as the energy of education and experience. I know what the tag classic means and I am reminded that I have achieved fame for my writing. A classic is a work of literature that transcends time and events. A classic lasts forever in time although some generations forget the virtues of a given book and adopt new vistas, new delights of reading. Some of the classics become old age and old fashion due to their lack of satisfying the need to be entertained. Some people are entertained by adventures and plots with unforgettable characters. Some are entertained by stories that have a satisfactory ending while some are entertained by the intellectualization of a work given to the exploration of ideas. Some readers expect spiritual appeasement of the soul in the quest of some form of enlightenment. A novel is a novel. It is predicated on the imagination spinning a story abounding in adventures and rich in unforgettable characters such as Don Quixote and Jean Valjean. I never intended to write classics. They became classics because I made them that way by sheer interest and a preference for the quality of text and characterization. What I conceived and then wrote down on paper is what turned out to be my writings that merited acclaim. People identified with what I wrote be it a particular character such as Ivanhoe or Lucie Ashton. They also enjoyed some adventures that seem to thrill them by their apparent bravery and Scottish charm. Rosa Bonheur liked my stories because they revived her sense of adventure and her feeling of being entertained while sitting in a chair waiting for the next adventure to unfold before her eyes and her mind imagining things and people that had been created for such and such a novel. She loved animals and she loved reading. She especially developed a liking, if not a love, for the Highlands that she visited with her friend, Nathalie Micas. The mind is not satisfied with tangible reality but also with intangible but created reality. I am not a philosopher nor am I a critic. I am a writer. That is why I am here with other writers in a sphere created for authors who, at times, suffered through and enjoyed during their lifetime the mastery of the art of good writing. By the way, I am Sir Walter Scott, the writer.

Now, let me talk about my books since I am flattered by the opportunity given to me after my death to discuss my writings. I must begin with my poems that I so enjoyed writing such as "Lady of the Lake" and others that people liked and read over and over again. I had always enjoyed reading beginning from an early age since I was left lame with a bout of polio and could not enjoy the sports that others participated in. I studied the classics when I was but twelve and was fascinated by the oral traditions, meaning stories told out loud while enjoying the warmth of a fire. These were stories handed down from generation to generation of the Scottish people and they truly captured my imagination and sense of belonging to a people that was rich in history and acts of bravery.

My novels are basically the documenting of my researches into the oral traditions of the Scottish Bodies in prose fiction. The first one was "Waverley", a tale of the Jacobite rising in 1745 in which the protagonist, like Don Quixote, is a great reader of romances. You see, the creative process of any man can be sent flying to the stars when rightly guided by the imagination. The protagonist is a man of divided loyalties and manages to separate himself from the division that shatters the loyalties of men. Then came what is called the Waverley novels and probably the better known one entitled, "The Bride of Lammermoor" in which we find the fated heroine, Lucie Ashton. The story was taken form actual history. Lucie Ashton is in love with the dispossessed and impoverished Edgar Ravenswood and they plan to wed. However, there are family disputes to reckon with and Lucie's mother forces her daughter to marry a wealthy man. Lucie is prey to a serious depression and on her wedding night stabs her husband and succumbs to insanity. This scene was rich in possibilities for a climatic coloratura mad scene of Donizetti's opera. I thank the composer for turning my story into an ever famous international piece of splendid music. Everyone will ever remember Maria Callas's rendition of the mad scene, one of her favorite arias I am told. You see, from oral story to a novel to an opera, that's how talent, briliant talent works, not that I call myself brilliant but at least notable in the eyes of the public.

Now, as for "Ivanhoe", the story is taken from the historic tale of the cruel tyranny of the Norman overlords over the impoverished Saxon populace of England. It's a shift from my more realistic novels in that I called it a "Romance." It is said that I reintroduced the Medieval values of the hero-knight. Ivanhoe returns from the Third Crusade with King Richard who goes incognito as the Black Knight or the Noir Faineant while Ivanhoe proclaims to be "Desdicado" the mysterious knight of the tournaments. That's right, I took full creative control of events in the Middle Ages such as tournaments, outlaws, witch trials, and the division between Jews and Christians to make it a story filled with adventures and historical happenings. I also introduced Gurth, Ivanhoe's knight's squire. Unlike Sancho Panza, he is an intelligent and wise person. All in all, I wanted to incorportae in my storytelling the attempt at unity between the Normans and the Saxons. The Normans in "Ivanhoe" represent a more sophisticated culture while the Saxons who are poor, disenfranchised and resentful of the Norman rule eventually band together to begin to mould themselves into one people. I'm not sure if the actual unity ever truly transpired completely. Even to this day, there are traces of disunity, at least, discord. Of course, there is more to the story but people will have to read the novel to better get a hold of all the components, especially the characters. Beside the plot or the intrigue as some call it, I created so many characters in this novel that for me it was like a giant puzzle with the pieces all coming together to form a whole. I must say that later assessment of my works was such that critics were part of the decline of my reputation as a writer since public and critical tastes changed from Romanticism to Realism. However, my stories remained pretty much in vogue and as classics no matter what the critics said. All I know is that my writings reflect the rich cultural history of the Highlands, and that is sufficient to preserve the spirit of Scotland and its traditions. The Waverley novels played a significant part in rehabilitating the public perception of the Scottish Highlands and its culture, which had been formally suppressed as barbaric, and viewed in the southern mind as a breeding ground of hill bandits, religious fanaticism, and Jacobite rebellions. I am so glad that I played a role in this, and that my writings are fresh and entertaining as ever. After all, literature is supposed to entertain and at times inspire, be they poems, plays, novels or any other pieces of world creative writings. I don't suppose that anyone would dispute that.

Before I forget, I promised Rosa Bonheur to allot time to her favorite poet and playwright, Edmond Rostand, especially to his play "Cyrano de Bergerac." This terrific play was a tremendous success in its heyday and continues to be so even to this day. It's the story of a man with a certain grotesqueness, that of a huge nose, who deploys his talent as a poet to woo and entertain the love of a friend, Roxanne. This friend is not capable of doing such poetic renditions. Rostand had long wanted to write a play based on his childhood hero, Cyrano de Bergerac, a 17th Century poet known for his refusal to conform and compromise. The part was played by the famous actor of his day, Constant Coquelin who incarnated Rostand's idea of this character whose ugly exterior would belie a noble soul. Coquelin did it to perfection as audiences applauded him unceasingl y. Rosa Bonheur loved this play since she felt much like the title character of Cyrano. That is the constant and commited refusal to conform and compromise. That, I believe was her trademark and her unfailing conviction to never cede to what is not right and unjust. At least in her own estimation of things.

"Monsieur Scott, it's now my turn, you know. Time to put in a few words, a few thoughts from a woman writer." "Yes, Madame Sand or should I say Madame Dupin?" "Whatever comes to your mind, my dear sir. Make way for a woman who decidedly modified the literary current of her times. Agree with me or not, I caused many rumors and raised eyebrows in my affairs with men. However, the important part of my being on earth, to me, was my writing. Rumors die and stories of personal lives vanish but good writing never fades away."

My name is Amantine-Lucie-Aurore Dupin better known as George Sand. Growing up, I was simply known as Aurore. I was raised by my grandmother on the Nohant estate in the French province of Berry. I grew up in a very liberal household. I got used to doing things my way, and challenged those who insisted that I do otherwise. You can say that I had a mind of my own. My grandmother was very indulgent towards me and favored my caprices. When I attained the age of being a young woman, I had learned to speak for myself, do whatever pleased me, and satisfied my every whim, be it a beautiful dress, a favorite chapeau that I had seen at the *coiffeuse,* a lovely pair of *chamois* cream-colored gloves or an evening out with my friends. I had many a friend both women and men. I loved men, especially the young gentlemen who were handsome and gay, especially those who had gained fame and a reputation as a writer or composer like Alfred de Musset and Frédéric Chopin. Now, there was a sickly man, Chopin. He had serious troubles with his lungs. His illness was aggravated when we visited Majorca. He was spitting blood and remained weak most of the time there. I loved the man and he loved me. He used to play some of his pianio compositions for me and even composed a very romantic melody for me, « Aurore. » That's what he called me, and not by married name of Dudevant. I had left my husband because I could not stand him any longer. He was a man of *aucune qualité sociale,* no social qualities, and of very modest means. So I picked up my two children and went away in my pursuit of a better and more enjoyable life. I wanted to live! But enough of my personal life. I must admit that I did enjoy the fruits of my various relationships with men that pleased me and knew how to please me in so many ways. I was stunned when I heard through the grapevine that some people called me *une putain manquée,* a lost whore. I wasn't a whore. I was a woman who needed and adored sensual pleasures in life. I was a bit like that Bovary woman that Gustave Flaubert invented for his grand novel. Flaubert and I were of different personalities and we sometimes quarreled but we remained friends. Good friends to the end. He had a great mind, Flaubert did, and he worked so very hard at his craft of style and *le mot juste.* I was always amazed at his passion for writing. He and I never had a love relationship. Of course, he had Louise Colet. What a troubled relationship these two had, but they stuck together. He wrote her piles of letters and she quite often answered them. She was his muse as he once told me. «Is that right, Gustave?». «Oui, Madame George.»

Enough of this. Let me tell you about my writing. First there's my pastoral novels based on my childhood days when I recognized the poor and often disenfranchised common man and woman. The laborer who toiled day and night to put food on the table. The people were often the target of the snobbish disdain of the upper class and given no privileges that could bolster their role in life. I felt genuine sympathy for them and I decided to base my first writings on their experiences and on their human worth. «La Mare au Diable» was the first of my *champêtre* or pastoral novels with «François le Champi» to follow suit, and then the other two « La Petite Fadette » and then « Les beaux Messieurs Bois-Doré. » « La Mare au Diable » is a favorite of mine, and I may add Rosa Bonheur's. It is said that she was inspired by the story for her painting "Ploughing in the Nivernais." I was and still am gratified to have given inspiration by one of my stories. Readers liked the touching story of Germain. Rosa Bonheur was right when she told a reader who was reading my story to her that I had to be fond of animals to write so about them with such feeling and reaslistic descriptions. I was fond of animals and fond of those who took good care of them. In the Berry region, there are many fine examples of good farmers and good women who earn their living by and through tilling of the soil they live on. It's not an easy living. As for my story of Germain, I preface it with an engraving by Holbein showing a man plowing the field, and I write about my commitment to esthetics and my writing so as to prove to the reader that I do have a sense of creativity and storytelling. My upbringing at Nohant gave me the opportunity to witness these peole who labored to plough the fields in the process of sharing their experiences in daily life. Writing to me was a labor of compassion and understanding of the mind and heart of these poor ordinary people who filled my mind and heart with their kindness, with their sense of morality and with their just and sincere view of the life on the land that was part of our province and our country that was France.

"La Mare du Diable" as you well know readers, is the story of Germain and Marie and how they get to be together on a journey to find a wife for the widower Germain as proposed by his father-in-law. I need not give you

all of the details of the story since you have read the story either in class or in private. It may have been read to you just as Proust's mother did when he was a child. What fascinates me is the "devil's pool" that is the title of the story. The reason behind it is the mysterious or magical wonder that is the pool. Is it the devil at work or a nefarious wonder that strikes the imagination without truly resolving the problem of identification or, as some say, symbolism. One can even see in the personages of Germain and Marie the knight and his damsel faced with the challenge of their plight as good people caught up with the dilemma of moral choices. Is the pond diabolical? Are the men chasing Marie evil? I leave that to the reader who needs challenges in reading stories. After all, the imagination needs to be nourished and developed.

Oh, I remember my preface so very well that I cannor help but to quote it right here. "Be careful, Madame George, not to extend your time and content," "There is no time here, Gustave." "But there is a reasonable allocation of a time element and you must not surpass it and deprive others of their time." "Let there be more time. This is Rosa Bonheur speaking and I do not usually like to interrupt, but I need to do it now." "Merci, chère dame *animalière.*"

Well, to quote my preface, not all of it of course: *Je venais de regarder longtemps et avec profonde mélancolie le laboureur d'Holbein, et je me promenais dans la campagne, rêvant à la vie des champs et à la destinée du cultivateur. Sans doute il est lugubre de consumer ses forces et ses jours à fendre le sein de cette terre jalouse, qui se fait arracher les trésors de sa fécondité lorsqu'un morceau de pain le plus noir et le plus grossier est, à la fin de la journée, l'unique récompense et l'unique profit attachés à un si dur labeur...* I had just contemplated at length and with profound melancholy Holbein's ploughman, and I was strolling through the countryside dreaming of the country life and the destiny of the one who cultivates the soil. Without doubt, it is a lugubrious thing to consume one's strength and days rending the bosom of this jealous soil from which is torn the treasures of its fecundity when a piece of bread, the darkest and the most gross is, at the end of the day, the unique recompense and the only profit attached to such a hard labor." Now, isn't that touching? I went on to say that I truly cared for the common laborer of the field and the common woman whose labor is as hard and gruesome as her husband's. Someone said that this was an idyllic tale of love and the open fidelity to the countryside and its traditional simplicity that many people ignored or even disdained. I know that it's somewhat of a romantic story but that is the way I conceived it. It also has elements of mysteriousness and possible withcraft mixed with the workings of the devil in his *mare du* diable,this devil's pond. I only wish that Holbein had also presented the angle of mercy and light, and not only the devil of death besides the poor ploughman. Is that the only recompense he deserves, death and the devil awaiting his every move? I do not think so, for love is the better recompense, and I like to write about that and not about some religious belief.

Now, as for "François le Champi", it's a good story, an exiciting reading for the young and old. However, I am not going to give you all of the details as I am not going to supply you with the details of my other two pastoral stories. You can read them and enjoy the fruits of my labor that are so much less arduous than those of the ploughman. Although, writing is not an easy labor. It takes time, energy and determination. *"Et la passion, Madame George." "Oui, Gustave."* One more word. I have seen and I have felt the beautiful in the simple, but to see and to depict are two different things. The most that the artist can hope to do is to induce those who have eyes to look with her. Look, my friends, look at what may astound you through your very own imagination and creativity. Finally, I must, for my sake, if not for the sake of all writers, that not all critics are on the right path when they denigrate a writer's efforts and accomplishments. Case in point, Charles Baudelaire when he said about me and my writings, "She is stupid, ponderous and garrulous. Her ideas on morals have the same depth of judgment and delicacy of feeling as those janitresses and kept women." There is more but I do not want to play in the vilest dirt with the man-poet. I must say that other writers did not see the way Baudelaire did. Although Flaubert never agreed with me on all things and though he was by no means an indulgent or forebearing critic, he was an admirer of mine and my work. So was Balzac, I must say. I knew him personally and he once said that if someone thought George Sand wrote badly it was because their own standards of criticism were inadequate. There! Take that and lump it you cannibal-critic Charles Baudelaire. "Here, here, Madame George, Enough of that." 'Yes, Mister Scott, Sir Walter Scott."I am just showing my feminine tendencies of willful strength that men did not recognize during my living."

Finally, I have to share this with my readers and those who have followed me and my career as a writer and especilaly as a woman.Yes, I was a person of will, determination and rebelliousnes in that I wore trousers and smoked tobacco in public, and called myself George. But that did not make me a slut or a woman of low moral values. I did what men were allowed to do just as Rosa Bonheur did except she did not smoke in public, only in private. She once said to her companion friend, the artist Anna Klumpke, and I quote. I can quote here in the sphere since it has been given to us to remember things that we did not usually remember so easily on earth. Here it is: "I venerate Madame Sand, and have only one reproach to make against her. She was too womanly, too kind, and dropped the treasures of her noble heart and the pearls of her soul on the dungheap, where the cocks found the pearls and swallowed them without being able to digest them." How is that for an answer to those who criticized me with an obdurate eye and a blackish heart. I was not immoral and am not now. I defer to the Creator to be my judge. No one else and certainly not men of twisted self-esteem who cannot even take the beam out of their own eyes. "*Cela suffit, Madame George* Sand...enough.." "*Oui, Gustave, cela suffit. Tu as raison comme toujours*...as always you are right." "*Attendez vous autres car Rosa Bonheur aura le dernier mot.*" "*C'est moi, l'animalière reconnue et forcément femme. Je ne peux pas laisser ce discours à la dérive du bon sens et de la justice. Madame Sand a été pour moi un exemple de fierté féminine et de prouesse chevalière devant les épreuves causées par des gens qui sont mal taillés, qui ont la tête mal vissée. Elle mérite notre estime le plus sincère et le plus frappant. C'est une vraie artiste. Chapeau, Madame Sand...* Wait you guys, for it is I Rosa Bonheur who will have the last word in this matter. I'm the animal painter, a well-known artist and forcibly a woman of strength and vital as well as creative energy. I will not let this discourse go adrift when it comes to good sense and justice. Madame Sand was for me an example of feminine pride and of chivalric prowess as was known yesteryear, an example of determination facing the trials caused by those who were badly put together and had their heads badly screwed on. She deserves our esteem the most sincere and the most striking of all. She is a true artist. Hats off to you Madame Sand. " "What can one say in this moment of truth and tenderness. It is I the author of this work and I take preference over all writers and creative members of the spheres since I am in control of this novel that is being written, want to or not. I need silence and a quiet moment of respite.

C'est le silence. Le grand silence monastique qui vient adouicir la peine du jour, la peine d'avoir à penser et à écrire sans mérite. It's the silence. The grand monastic silence that comes to soften the pain of having to think and to write without merit. SILENCE...le repos du silence.

CHAPTER TWELVE

Well, here we are at this phase of my novel. There are other writers who claim their right to appear in this novel, but I cannot cede to them for I would have to write hundreds and hundreds of pages, if not thousands to satisfy all writers. Can you imagine all of the writers in historic earthly time, of all categories, of all nations, of all languages? It would be an impossible task. Readers would not tolerate such a lengthy book. So, I limit myself to a few who have had some measure of influence on Rosa Bonheur's life. After all, this is a work on her life and artistic achievements. It is not a compendium of eternal and everlasting writings. Some will survive the ravages of time and the sting of forgetfullness, if not oblivion, while others will go on living in our memory and our delight in being entertained and inspired by and with literature, and, of course, music. How about the sciences, some may ask. What about the sciences? Enough has been said and done about the sciences from my point of view. Not that they are not important factors in human lives but they have their very own outlets of distribution and discovery, and need not take away from the humanities what is due them. Although, the greatest of scientists are the people of the humanities. I mean, they are consecrated to them be it, philosophy, theology, literature, history, music, culture and languages, all aspects of the humanities. Take the great DaVinci and Einstein, for example. What better example of well-formed and creative minds discovering the power of the scientific motion and construction of the world surpassing time and space. They were formed by the great queries of the humanities. When the man or woman of science is more attached to the humanities as a bird is linked inextricably to the wind in the skies above, then he or she becomes a better person, a more educated person who has learned how to really fly. In order to fly, a bird must have wind and wings. In order to soar as a person, a man or a woman must have the spirit of the holistic formation of mind and soul. Yes, to soar is to reach the stars when others stay planted there with their two feet stuck in the mud. Physics and mathematics may give you the key to so many problems of the earth and sky, but literature and music and all of the other disciplines of the humanities can open the doors of knowing oneself and plunging into life with the gusto of passion and the vitality of being fully and truly alive. A single line of poetry, one well-turned metaphor and one a well-constructed phrase or musical score can entirely redirect you to the key of the fullness of living. If you cannot experience this and get the primal juices of what is life and the patterns of living, then you are not whole. You are missing something very important and quite possibly vital in your life. The energy of the soul without which there is no true life, only death in the soul. Calculations, problem resolutions, algebraic equations, and quantum theories and whatever the mind conceives scientifically will not suffice to keep the fire of full life going. Fires go out. They smolder and slowly die. They need to be kept alive. So does the fire of the soul. It needs to be kept burning with the fire of passion and creativity. The spiritual dimensions of the humanities can do that. Only the will to live and to take the breath of the lofty air of poetry and music can inspire the soul to go beyond the limits that one creates for himself and for others. I adhere to Einstein's way of thinking when he says that scientific thought and quantifications can only be modified by access to the creative soul or as he says, the spirit of the human being grasping the very principles of life and the imagination. "Knowledge is limited. Imagination encircles the world," he once said. Other scientists such as Noah Chomsky and Maria Konnikova are of the same thought when it comes to art and humanities. They tell us to stop fitting everything, every thought, every conceivable creation to a neat model that succumbs to statistical analysis. Noam Chomsky speaks of the value of the novel in that it leads us to better understand human life and human personality. And there are so many more scientists who recognize the value of art and humanities in conjunction with the sciences. The scientific mind cannot, should not exclude the power of the imagination that helps us human beings to create and appreciate the holistic approach to everything we can imagine. Rational thought is only one component of the human dimension. I personally would prefer to choose to live with Mozart and Shakespeare rather than with a scientist who rules out everything that is part of the creative imagination. People tell me oftentimes to be more practical. I am. I think in terms of the practicality of the human mind linked to the product of my imagination, and I marvel at what I have accomplished in my life as a human being. Practicality leaves us standing on firm ground while a leap from practicality leaves me soaring to the heavens where angels abide, the angels of pure delight who inspire me to appreciate the arts, music, literature, culture, philosophy, theology and so many more facets of knowledge and soul disciplines. Why, I can be inspired and learn to indulge in the mystique of a single poem while a banal equation can only make me smile and look away. The girl with the pearl earring in Vermeer's painting draws me closer to reality than the pearl earring in a jewelry store. Why? Because Vermeer's earring bring me that closer to myself as a human being and as a person appreciating the joys af art.

Enough of this, my readers, for I could go on for days and nights and still not reach my goal of convincing the many thinkers and creators out there. "*Cela suffit, Monsieur l'auteur...*that's enough." "Who said that?" It is I MOZART. It's time for the composers of music and harmony that fill the mind and soul with the mysteries of pleasant and fulfilling sounds that opens up the soul to its full capacity and makes the listener attentive to the various hamonies that attend the soul. So many people do not want to listen to me when I speak of music and the soul, but I am right on this point. Music and soul are the holistic dimensions of human life in gestation. For we as human beings are never complete until we harness the energy of the soul and soar to infinity. Death never finishes off life. It only separates the mortal from the immortal, and music is immortal.

Yes, it is I Wolfgang Amadeus Mozart, the composer musician of long ago. However, my music is still very much alive today. I come here from this other sphere where we composers and musicians are relegated to because I have been called to make a testimony on Rosa Bonheur's life and artistic achievements. Why, would you ask? Because Rosa Bonheur was a devotee of my music and she appreciated listening to my sonatas and operas.

People always wondered when I started to compose music, at four, five or six years old? Earlier than that. I was hearing music in my head when I was a few months old but could not put it down on paper. I heard music, those harmonies that resounded in my very young mind, and I enjoyed them as if they were the sounds of angels. I believe now that they were sounds of angels that were inspiring me to grow with music and harmonies. The Creator sent his angels to inspire me in order to show humanity that music was an integral part of one's education. To be educated meant to be formed in the disciplines that form the mind and soul. The link with the angels is the sign that what I experienced was in great part divine. I owe my music to the divine element. It grew in me through inspiration that was inculcated in my mind and soul. You have to have soul in music for it's not just notes on a manuscript. Music of the spheres is what they call my music. I call it music of the night. Nighttime is a time for relaxation and inspiration when the silence of the night reinforces your drive to compose and to pray. Yes, I prayed and that helped me stay on line with divine inspiration. Where else does inspiration come from if not from the spheres? That's where I'm at now, the spheres of the composers and musicians. Everything that is creativity is inspiration when you come to the very core of creativity. My music was my life and my life was my music. I thrived on it and it gave me the strength to live on and produce what was best in my life, the talent for music. I did not waste it for some people waste their talent by scurrilously abandoning it or by the *effritement*, the erosion of talent and music. I did not seek fame but rather acknowledgment. Certainly I needed money to live on and support my family, but I did not seek money for the sake of money. I loved life and its pleasures for sure, and I did not hide my penchant for what pleased me. I was ever the sensuous being in life. My body and all of my senses were part of my way of being alive, fully alive. I thought that I deserved these pleasures for I worked hard at my craft. The craft of music-making is a difficult one although I never found it to be hard. It just flowed as day and night flow in your life. My best time was nighttime. How I loved the night. That's when my best inspiration came to me. Night is the venue of the angels. I could hear their voices in my head, the voices of heavenly music, or as I called it the music of the spheres. Music can be so heavenly, inspirational and divine. It soothes the soul and clears the mind or every tedious worry and problem that creep up into your life during the daytime hours. The silence of the night is the silence of the soul and that's why music is part of that silence. Silence is not total absence of sounds. No, it's the total absorption of the sounds of music in your mind and soul. That's the way I see it. You may find me odd and somewhat mad, but that's me. Mozart the madman. Madness is a way of acknowledging human weaknesses, and I had many of them but not in the realm of music. What is madness anyway, a loss of reality? a loss of intellectual capacities? a loss of connectedness? a loss of one's right behavior? a loss of being able to know what is right from wrong? No. It's not any of those things. Not exactly. In my mind, it's not a loss but a gain of passion since passion can take over the mind and its intellectual capacities. I can say that, at times, my passion for music did take over me and my capacities to think straight. However, I gained in creativity and stubborn pride that made me think twice about my composing music. Was Christ mad when he jumped into his passion and did what was considered stupid and mad by people he knew, even his disciples? No, he was not simply mad but in his pursuit of his passion, the passion of the cross and of salvation. That's the way I see it and the way others do. We each have a trajectory of passion and we can take it and do something with it or reject it and go downhill where the lost dreams are piled up as a result of frustrations and the denial of talent to create. My mind always denied the presumption of greatness based on false pretensions of creativity. All I ever did was to uncover layer by layer the possibilities of creativity and immersed myself in the inspiration that was being given to me. *Carpe diem!* Yes, seize the day for life is short...*Ars longa, vita brevis*, yes, art is long when life is so short as I have experienced it myself. I died at a young age on account of some illness that even the doctors could not diagnose. Then, I was buried in the common grave and my bones were lost with time. That's alright as long as my music remains eternal. Can one imagine what I could have done with a few more years added to my life? Unimaginable and inconceivable. I could have composed my greatest music in that time lost on earth. I know many of you claim that my music is great, but it could have climbed the very highest of summits of composition given the chance to expand my musical qualities and perceptions. I'm convinced that my inspiration would have expanded beyond what I had already received in angelic terms, but it was not given to me to extend my life on earth. As I lay dying while my wife, Constanze and her youngest sister were attending Doctor Closset hoping to rescue me from death, I saw the whirling of a musical vortex taking me up and up and up toward the spheres where I am now situated but cannot be inspired to compose music any longer, for my creativity has been cut short by death. I am no longer a human being alive but a soul wandering in the spheres with the magnificent brightness of the stars. So, all of you out there in the world, compose, write, paint, read with passion and especially listen to your creative soul. And, listen attentively to my music. It's worth a few moments of your time and energy to conceive, no, to grasp, greatness in action. Greatness does not impose itself on you, it comes with the genius that is inspired in your soul. The genius to create and inspire others to do the same.

Now, let's get down to music, my music. Rosa Bonheur loved my Piano Sonata No. 16 in C major. I call it a "sonata for beginners" or **Sonata facile**. Anyone can play this one. She especially liked the Allegro part. Well, I can say that this sonata is easily identifiable with my name, Mozart. It has a quality to it that is simple yet complex in its variety of notes. It was so easy for me to compose this sonata. It came to me as if in a dream and when I awoke there it was bright and clear in tone and musicality. Now, some of you may be thinking that the author of this novel is not transcribing my thoughts and words correctly, and that Mozart would not use such thoughts and words in analyzing his music. Well, I trust the author and I think he is doing an excellent job, for it is not an easy task to transcibe someone else's thoughts and words concerning music, especially when he does not know too much music. He's learning and learning fast, that's all I have to tell you.

As for sonatas, I must say that most peole who know some music and especially my music, know that a sonata has three parts, the Allegro, the Andante, and the Rondo. The Allegro offers the tempo and the development of the theme while the Andante has a slower movement. The Rondo is the finale which means that it closes the sonata. I always chose the three movements while Hadyn sometimes chose three and sometimes four. That was his choice.

I also had church sonatas, "sonatas de chiesa" as they were called. They were played at the celebration of the Mass between the Epistle and the Gospel. They made a lovely and meditative transition between the two readings. However, shortly after I left Salzburg, the Archbishop mandated that an appropriate choral motet or congregational hymn be sung at that point in the liturgy and the "Epistle Sonata" fell into disuse. He was a cunning and somewhat vengeful man, the Archbishop was.

Now, let me talk about concertos. I composed more than twenty-seven concertos for piano and orchestra. Many were composed for myself since I wanted to play them in the Vienna concert series. You all know what a concerto is so I won't have to describe it to you and waste time. However, I must say that I made a decisive advance in the organization of the first movement as I did in my early concerto "Jeunehomme No.9". I insisted that the piano retain its ancient keyborad *basso continuo* role in the orchestral *tuttis* of the concertos. And, I liked to improvise as everyone knows. Improvisation is the hallmark of an enlightened artist. Improvisation is the embellishment of the piano as written in the score. I thought I would add that for those who wonder what my improvisations were. Concertos were the means by which I entertained and delighted audiences. In a letter to my father, most of which I remember word for word, I tell him about the pleasure of composing and performing concertos as well as the reception these compositions received: "These concertos[Nos. 11,12,13] are a happy medium between what is too easy and too difficult; they are very brilliant, pleasing to the ear, and natural without being vapid. There are passages here and there from which the connoisseurs alone can derive satisfaction, but these passages are written in such a way that the less learned cannot fail to be pleased, though without knowing why...The golden means of truth in all things is no longer either known or appreciated. In order to win applause one must write stuff which is so inane that a coachman could sing it, or so unitelligible that it pleases precisedly because no sensible man can understand it." There you have it, my ode to concertos.

I must add that I managed to create a unique conception of the piano concerto that attempted to solve the ongoing problem of how thematic material is dealt with by the orchestra and the piano. I strove to maintain a means between a symphony with occasional piano solos and a virtuoso piano fantasia with orchestral accompaniment. My resulting solutions were varied and, I may add, complex. Now, have I mystified or even confused some of you? I hope not. However, it's time I speak of my operas, an important phase in my career as a composer musician. "It is I, Georges Bizet, who is talking to you. I realize that you played an important role in the world of music and we are all grateful to you, and I enjoy being here with you in this sphere of departed composers and musicians, but I need to have some time too. I knew Rosa Bonheur and I even composed a lovely melody for her...so please make it short Amadeus." "Short? I cannot shorten my time for my operas but I will make it brief and to the point. However, I will not allow anyone to push me into an encroachment of my work. Never." "Please allow him the gentility to proceed with some of the finest operas ever composed." "You, Massenet, you have to butt in, don't you. You composers of romantic operas are all the same, flighty, stubbornly proud, and right down meddlesome. Oh, alright, get on with it my dear Mozart. I defer to your palpable genius." "Merci, my dear Bizet. You are so very discerning when it comes to musical talent. By the way, I love your *Pêcheurs de Perles* . There are moments of French genius in it, brief but rare." "Don't get me going, my Salzburg sausage."

It is I, Mozart, who now has the floor although there are no floors over here. Ha! Ha! Now, here I am again with my music and the opera. What a hard but enjoyable work is the opera. First you have to find a librettist, a knowledgeable and talented one. I found one in Lorenzo Da Ponte. He wrote the libretto for my opera "Don Giovanni." What an opera and what a moral tale of a seducer and libertine. He suffers the same fate as Faustus. The opera premiered at the Teatro di Praga where there were no opera lovers like the citizens of Prague. They respond so very well to my music. It's an *opera buffa* blending comedy, melodrama and supernatural elements. The overture begins with a thundering D minor cadence, followed by a short *misterioso* sequence which leads into a light-hearted D major allegro. I planned everything that I wrote on paper and even, at times, improvised, to make the whole more perfect to my taste and talent. I love the hero, this Don Giovanni, based on the Spanish Don Juan. He's a young arrogant and sexually promiscuous nobleman who outrages everyone with his words and actions. A man after my own heart. He is unfaithful to everyone, especially women, and has an entire list of conquests to his name. When he meets the Commandatore, the father of the woman he is about to seduce, sparks fly and a duel ensues so that the Commandatore is killed by Don Giovanni's sword.

It is a very difficult opera to fully understand, but it is worthwhile appreciating the music that enraptured the audience in Prague and so many more after that. If you follow the plot and every detail of the opera, you discover that it was well constructed and very well scored. I know, I did it with passion and talent. I'm not going to relate all of the details of the opera. That would take too much time that I do not have. However, I want to stress the supernatural elements of the opera and the statue of the Commandatore come to life who is invited to dinner by the young scroundrel where he tells him *"Don Giovanni! A cenar teco m'invitasi...*you invited me to dine with you. The statue offers him the last chance to repent but Don Giovanni resoundly refuses. The statue disappears and Don Giovanni cries out in pain and terror surrounded by a chorus of demons to drag him into hell. What a scene! What an extravagant melodrama that comes to an end with gusto. Don Giovanni goes to hell in a dazzling coup de théâtre. Can you imagine a statue singing in an opera? *Un tour de force.* Other composers liked my opera to a point that they tried to imitate my work in their own way such as Franz Liszt, Chopin, Beethoven and even Tchaikovski. He's the one who said as he gazed at the manuscript that he was "in the presence of divinity." Now, that's praise for you. Recognition of a great work of art. "I'm going to chime in, I, Flaubert, who once said that Don Giovanni along with Hamlet were the finest things God ever made." *"Merci, Monsieur Flaubert."*

Let us move on, shall we? "When do I get my chance?" "Bizet, hold on, your turn will come." *"Pourquoi m'ont-ils mis dans un endroit où les plein-paroles m'entourent?...*why did they place me with people who talk all the time?" "You only have me for a little while and then I shall disappear like the Commandatore's statue." "Oh, shut up with your statue and your coup de théâtre. It's all so very melodramatic." "But it worked."

The next opera I want to talk about is the one Rosa Bonheur liked, "Le nozze di Figaro." It premiered in Vienna. It's a simple story of a philandering employer Count Almaviva, his wife, the Countess, Figaro and Susanna. It's called in French *la folle journée,* a single day of madness at court. It's a love story complicated by a count who wants to exercise his feudal right, *le droit du seigneur,* the right of the lord to bed his servant on her wedding night. Figaro is fuming at the thought of such lunacy, and the opera unfolds with its arias and with its music to make people delirious with applause and delight. It's a happy-ending tale with the disguised Countess reunited with her Count. She forgives him for his meddling in the love and marriage of Figaro and Susanna. The overture is in the key of D major, the tempo marking is *pesto*, fast and lively. I used the sound of two horns playing together to represent the cuckoldry in the opera. Overall, it's a profound tale of love, betrayal and forgiveness. I simply loved it and that's why I decided to write the score that truly embellished the tale. The lively and intricate ensemble scenes won over the hearts of so many who witnessed the opera over the years, I am told. The music is well crafted and immensely sophisticated, someone once told me, and I thanked him for his praises. Johannes Brahms said that "each number in Figaro is a miracle. It is totally beyond me how anyone could create anything so perfect." Imagine! Joseph Hadyn appreciated the opera greatly. So there you have it.

I'd like to continue on and speak of "Cossi Fan Tutti" but I'm afraid I would be overstepping my welcome into this sphere of composers and musicians. However, I have to say a few words about the jewel of my operas, "Die Zauberflöte", "The Magic Flute." It's a gem of an opera with magic, mysterious and symbolic moments that challenge the mind and soul of participants. It is a participatory event and it challenges those who would delve into the symbolism of every note and of every word. I just tell people to enjoy "The Magic Flute" because it's meant to entertain. Enjoy the music. Enjoy the Queen of the Night's coloratura aria where she must reach a high F which is rare in operas. I did it on purpose to challenge the soprano's voice and those divas who can reach such a high note. I love challenges like that. I also love the two lovers, the prince and the princess and especially the bird-catcher. The Bird-Catcher song is reminiscent of folk songs, and I gave it folk-like melody. It's a fairy tale blended with folk music that reach out to people, and they loved it. Remember that I did not compose only for the high society people but also for the common man and the common woman who come to operas to be entertained. I did it for the men and women of the times in my and their native language which is German. Yes, "The Magic Flute" is a jewel of culture and fable mixed with the my most challenging effort that I ever made for operatic music.

It received silent approval from the audience and that made me very proud of my accomplishment. Not too long afterwards, I passed away leaving behind my wife with the only treasure I could leave behind, my music. I am so proud of my music and it has influenced so many other composers that I do not know what to say any more. Music of the spheres, as they say.

Well, now is my turn, at last. My name is Georges Bizet, baptized as Alexandre César Léopold. I am a French composer as most people know. They know me as the composer of the opera "Carmen" but I also composed other music such as *Les Pêcheurs de Perles, La Jolie Fille de Perth,* and *L'Arlésienne.* I'm here because I want to say that I rendered homage to Rosa Bonheur when she received the Legion of Honor. I wrote for her a lovely musical number called *"La rose impériale.* It was a melody based on the great honor that she had recently received.

I know that most people know me for my opera "Carmen" and it's a frightfully lively piece of music with gypsy overtones that crackle and spark and send the audience in a frenzy, the frenzy of melodies not soon forgotten. Carmen is a gypsy witch and she easily seduces, and that's why I gave Don José the romantic song *"La fleur que tu m'avais jetée,* a melody that charms and goes right to the heart of the seduced one. And, of course, everyone remembers the "Gypsy Song" with its swirling highly frenzied melody. And, finally the "Toreador Song" that enchants so many to a point of joining in like a triumphal march. However, the melody that I most cherish is the one from *Les Pêcheurs de perles, " Au fond du temple saint"* a charming and sweet-sounding duet by a tenor and a baritone. This opera with its exotic Oriental setting still lingers in my heart. Concerning Mozart, I may tease him and call him a sausage, but I must admit that he was a man of genius, although I once said that Mozart's music affected me too deeply and made me really unwell. I do not know why. "That's because you never fully understood my music, Georges." "Mozart, please do not interrupt. I have enough thinking of my own music and my career that was cut short." "So was mine, Georges, so was mine."

S'il-vous-plaît, mon tour, my turn. My name is Jules Émile Frédéric Massenet. The French love to give a series of names at baptism recognizing not only the names of saints but those of specific relatives dear to them. I have loved music since I was a child. So when I was older, I knew that I had been predestined for music and besides becoming a musician, I learned to compose music and operas. I was told that I had a good sense of the theater. I loved the stage, the settings, the scenery, the decor, the overall enchantment of the theater and especially the charm of music rising above the footlights and reaching the audience eagerly awaiting the soothing sounds, the passionate sounds, the vibrant sounds, the thrilling sounds of the voices singing the librettos caught on the script by the composer. I was going to be the creator of all of the making of an opera from the initial story to the last note on the last page. I had the creative ability to do that and I was going to spend my life doing it. And, that's what I did. Some people said that my operas as well as my music in general was the old-fashioned and unadventurous products of la Belle Époque. I let them say what they thought, I didn't care. I was going to compose music and my music would be the genuine expression of my creative soul. It would be genuine, real, transparent in its sentiments, and spiritually conceived or soul-inspired. That's what I thought then. I was right about it being genuine since it came from the deepest sensuous fibers of my body and all of the heavings of my soul. I suppose that's why some people said that I had the gift of suave and voluptuous melody. I suppose I did, and I marveled at people recognizing this gift in me.

I wrote so many pages of music in my career as a composer but what I'm really proud of are my operas. To name some, there is *Manon, Le Cid, Werther, Don Quichotte,* and *Thaïs.* You see, Senor Cervantes, I did borrow from your magnificent and entertaining story of the knight chasing windmills and pursuing his illusionary affection for Dulcinea. As for *Manon,* almost everyone knows the story and the music since it has been staged in so many opera houses. I was told that Rosa Bonheur loved this opera and attended a performance while in Paris. The Saint Sulpice scene is one of the most memorable ones that I composed for opera. As for *Werther it* is a tender story of crushed love, a doomed love on the part of a young poet's love for the beautiful Charlotte. I relied on Goethe's tragic story that became very popular in his lifetime. Werther's suicide due to the unattainable love for Charlotte is a sad and tragic ending to my opera. It's deeply romantic and at the same time existentially real. At first, people did not seem to appreciate this opera but it came into acceptance later on. As far as *Don Quichotte* is concerned, well, everyone knows the adventures of Don Quixote and Sancho Panza as Senor Cervantes wrote it to the marvel of all those who read the novel and delighted in it. I stress the role of Dulcinea in my opera. The windmill scene is there and Don Quixote's affirmation that he is the Knight-errant, *Je suis le chevalier errant.* He is a dreamer and a person of many illusions that are woven in his life. In my opera, Don Quixote is a man of the stars and of Medieval knightly adventures that the poor man has read in so many romances. I think I kept the core meaning of the story and, Senor Cervantes, you can be proud of my musical adaptation. " *Estoy tan orgulloso de ti, senor Massenet.*" I am proud of your work. *Merci, Senor Cervantes. Vous êtes de la classe des justes et des brilliants écrivains...*You are of the class of the just ones and the brilliant writers."

Now, as for my opera *Thaïs,* I have a special fondness for this work. I was told that Rosa Bonheur loved the "Meditation" scene and its solo. She used to ask her friend, Anna Klumpke, to enjoy listening to this music with her when some of her neighbors in Thomery came to play the "Meditation" on violin and flute for her. Rosa Bonheur was not a romantic person but she did shed a tear or two while listening to this music, for she told her friend, Anna, that was because it reminded her of her beloved mother whom she missed so very much. *Thaïs* is the story of a courtesan vowed to the cult of Venus who encounters a monk with a passion for salvation. He begs her to give up her life as a sinner and sends her off to a convent where she undergoes conversion. However, he is madly in love with his so-called creation of the converted child and goes to the convent to proclaim his passionate love for Thaïs. His obsession is rooted in lust, and he tells her that heaven is not real, only love is in order to claim her and her love. But, she affirms in a dream-like stage that she sees heaven opening up to her. Very similar to Gounod's scene of Marguerite's apotheosis in his opera "Faust". I did not plagiarize his scene but was inspired by it, and I introduced this part of the opera into my work along with the symphonic intermezzo, "Meditation", that has become revered by many who simply love what they call divinely inspired music. I know I'm being sentimental about this, but that's what I conceived and that's what I share with all of my followers. Now, I realize that I have not given you too many details of my operas, but I did not want to make it a documentary of all my works. I'm a humble and even a shy man, and I do not want to show myself as a proud peacock with its feathers all swollen as if in a fan. No, I want my music to speak for me and for itself. I know many people consider my music and my operas to be too sugary and perhaps too romantic of the Belle Époque days, but that's the way it is, and that's the way it will stay, for there is nothing I can do about it now. *Je suis un revenant,* I am a ghost of the spheres.

Readers, what about other noted writers and composers such as Victor Hugo, Guy de Maupassant, Baudelaire, for instance. How about Hadyn, Beethoven, Bach and so many other great composers, you may ask. Well, this novel is not a compendium of all writers and composers, as I have said before. I have to keep this work in line with my main idea of subject matter, Rosa Bonheur. I only use the writers and composers that affected or influenced, in some way, Rosa Bonheur's life and career as an artist. Now, where do we go or rather where do I go from here, is the big question. We are going nowhere except the spheres of the creative spirits that have molded the lives of so many artists like Rosa Bonheur. But we have already gone there in the last chapter, you will say. Yes, but not the sphere of the spirit of animals, the animals that the *animalière* Rosa Bonheur so loved and admired for their beauty and natural intelligence. Animals? You may ask. Yes, animals have lives of creativity and a spirit and personality all their own. Are they completely dead? Not exactly, not dead but alive in the spheres of our imagination and creativity. "Wait a minute." "Yes, Monsieur Bizet. What is it? "I want to know if we the artists of the spheres are also imaginary?" "Remember that the imagination is creative and that reality exists even it's a product of the imagination. So, all of you are alive in the creative imagination of all of us here on earth. You are not totally defunct." "How about heaven and hell? Purgatory?" "That's another dimension of living and dying, Monsieur Bizet. I will not go that way. It's beyond my reach as a writer seeking truth in the making. I will let other authors do that if they so wish. Not I. I am here to explore and invent the reality around Rosa Bonheur's career as an artist and as a person who loved animals. An artist who painted so many animals in her liftetime that she is recognized for her skill as an artist of great talent. Besides, I wanted a subject for my new book since I was running out of ideas." "All you writers are all the same. You keep running out of ideas until you are hit on the head by a new or even outlandish thought that you want to pursue as subject matter for a new book. Life is not a book." "I know but what would you do without books?" "Compose more music, I suppose." "Come on, Bizet, what would you really do without books? You need inspiration to compose and write the libretto." "I, Mozart, could not survive without the inspiration of certain books coupled with the inspiration of the stars." AMEN. "Thank you, beloved Mozart, thank you. You have spoken the words of a true artist. The world of artists and composers, as well as writers like me, owe you a debt of gratitude." "Gratitude is never refused, *mein Herr.*"

CHAPTER THIRTEEN

Readers, let us travel to the sphere where the *animalière* Rosa Bonheur sends us whirling in her creative imagination, the sphere of animals long gone but never extinct like her dear Fathma that she so loved.

All right. Here we are the departed animals of Rosa Bonheur's paintings and sketches. Yes, we can talk since in this imaginary and creative world, or should I say sphere. We have been given the power of hearing, listening and, Oh God! even talking like human beings. Can you imagine? The author has created this sphere so we can communicate with his readers, and find out more about Rosa Bonheur.

Here we are in the sphere of the animals who will entertain you with their earthly adventures, and narrate for us the marvelous stories that affected the life of the one artist who changed the way we look at animals in the creative imagination of artists and onlookers who appreciate art and the animal world. Ladies and gentlemen, I give you ROSA BONHEUR.

Yes, here I am once more. I am here to entertain you about the vast possibilities of the animal kingdom, wild and tame. I know that a lot has transpired since I first spoke to you readers. I am pleased with the author's offerings about the creative artists who touched my life, writers and composers. Merci! However, what is most important to me as an artist is the fact that animals became an integral part of my life and my career as a creative artist. Without them I could not have gone beyond portrait painting and copying masterpieces in the Louvre and other museums. I owe my life and career to animals. Now, some of you may think that I became infatuated with animals simply to make money and enjoy life and its pleasures. Nothing further from the truth, I tell you. Sure, I needed to earn a living and make ends meet, but I did not paint to earn piles of money and gain fame by doing so. No. First of all, I had to learn my craft that eventually became my art. My true, sincere and solidly identifiable art, and they called me an *animalière*. That's alright since I do not care what they call me as long as they appreciate the hours, days, and even years that I put nto my work. I know the effort and energy that I put into it. I know. *J'ai coulé des heures et des heures là-dedans.Vous ne saurez jamais tous les efforts que moi, Rosa Bonheur, ai mis dans mes oeuvres. Ce fut tout un boulot de cultivateur, je vous l'assure, car le cultivateur doit cultiver la terre and la remettre en état de semence et de fructification, et ça, ça prend de l'énergie et un effort parfois surhumain. C'est la même chose avec l'écriture et la peinture. George Sand peut vous l'admettre sans fin...*I put in hours and hours of hard work in it. You will never know all the effort that I, Rosa Bonheur, put into my works as an artist. It was a hell of hard work like the farmer who farms his land by cultivating it so that the soil be rendered ready for sowing and fruition again. That takes energy and a great effort, at times superhuman effort. It's the same thing with writers and painters. George Sand knows a few things about it."

Enough of my talking and now is the time to share some of my experiences with the animals that I painted by making them talk about their side of the story.

I'm Fathma, the beloved lioness of Rosa Bonheur. She claimed that I was so *apprivoisée,* tamed, that I used to follow her like a poodle. She truly loved me and I satisfied her love for animals the best way I could by lavishing on her my love and affection. When an animal such as I receive love like the love Rosa Bonheur offered me, that animal becomes attached to any person who is so loving and lovable. We have feelings too, we animals. I was privileged to have found a person like Rosa Bonheur, this *animalière* who understood animals and loved them the best way she could by being honest in her feelings and transparent in her intentions of caring for all of us. That is why I responded to her love the way I did and so did the many animals in her menagerie. I still feel her pain and mourning after she found me dead at the foot of the stairs at Chateau de By. That was quite a blow to her. Rosa Bonheur used to play with me in her spare time which was not much since she was so busy sketching and painting. She even let me lie down on her bed, not under the covers but right on this huge comforter that she kept on her bed. She was often so cold this lady, *frileuse,* she used to say. She did not have *un lion*, a man, to keep her warm. I'm just kidding. Rosa Bonheur was a woman who laughed all the time. She was seldom sad or grumpy. She sure was sad when I died and had an empty spot in her heart. Well, every creature dies at one time or another, you know that. We are not immortal, we animals, but we live on in the minds and hearts of those who knew us and loved us. And we exist in the sphere of the revenant animals. I would like Pierrette, the other lioness, to talk to you about Rosa Bonheur, but she doesn't feel up to it. She's a strange one that one. She has never felt comfortable up here in this sphere since she passed away years ago. She's full of remorse for having left the earth and its comfort, as she calls it. I don't. I'm happy up here in the clouds or should I say the spheres.

Hello. I'm Boniface one of Rosa Bonheur's monkeys. Yes, she even kept monkeys in her menagerie of all kinds of animals. We monkeys were given the full run of the house, and we delighted in it. Quite often, Miss Anna tried to shoo us away but Rosa Bonheur told her to let us be except when we were really bad like the time I dropped a vase on the tile floor and it broke. However, she did not punish me for it . She said that vases could be replaced. I hid under her bed for a whole day thinking that she would run after me to give me hell. She often reported our mischiefs to her friends for she liked our little episodes of *singerie,* "monkeyishness". Ratata, another monkey used to like to play in Rosa Bonheur's hair, can you imagine? She told one of her friends that she thought that Ratata took her for an old male of her kind.

We cannot forget the sheep, the ewes and the rams but especially the lambs. I am a sheep among many other sheep that saw Rosa Bonheur gaze at us for a very long time in order to sketch what she was going to paint later on, like the boat full of sheep being transported to another pasture. So many other paintings of sheep that one would have to keep track of all of them in order to define the best painting of sheep. One that I can easily single out is the head of a lamb, my little baby, my love. Yes, I'm a ewe, a sheep who had many children but remembers one in particular, the one that Rosa Bonheur painted and still lives on in the annals of fine arts. That painting is a memorable one, one that Rosa Bonheur particularly liked and treasured. I can see it now, the realisitc head of a lamb with the whitest of wool and soft eyes that a mother like me cannot resist. Unfortunately, lambs grow up like people, and I lost my lamb in the shuffle of movement and sales. However, I will always remember my lamb because he has been immortalized by the talented *animalière* that was, rather is, Rosa Bonheur.

Then there was the deer, specifically the doe and her fawn. I am that doe who trained her fawn to love nature and seek happiness in the things of nature. It was simply natural to be in nature and to love nature and depend on nature. Only in nature were we the true creatures of the Great Creator. Men hunted us, poachers robbed us of our natural settings, while other human beings took care of us and gave us the freedom to roam in the wild. Rosa Bonheur loved us in a way so as to guarantee our freedom and allow us to enjoy the freedom of the wild and free lands such as the Fontainebleau forest. She would occasionally come to see us and make sketches of me and my fawn, just so she could later on paint us on canvas. I knew that she would make a very good realistic painting of the doe and her fawn, and I let her gaze at us without moving an inch so that she could do her art work at ease. I admired her and her passion for animals, and I let her know by my glance that I appreciated her dedication to wild animals like me and my fawn. That is all I have to say.

Well, it's time for the horses to chime in. First there's Solferino, the black stallion who was one of Rosa Bonheur's favorites. He was named after the color Solferino, a moderate purplish-red color and not after the battle of Solferino when Napoleon III along with the Sardinian Army under Victor Emmanuel II fought against the Austrian Army and won the battle. Rose Bonheur loved her Solferino.

Yes, Rosa Bonheur loved me and my fine and shiny coat along with my dark silken mane. I rode her to town quite often, and she enjoyed riding horseback when the thought of riding in the Fontainebleau forest took a hold of her enough to leave her work behind, saddle me up and go riding long hours into the dark forest. I didn't care as long as she took good care of me and did not abuse me. She loved all animals but I think that horses like myself were her very favorites. Of course, I must not forget the lions. "Don't ever forget lions, Solferino." "No, Fathma, I will not for Rosa Bonheur never did put lions aside. She loved you to a point of infatuation."

This time it's me, Panther, Rosa Bonheur's mare. How she spoiled me and took care not to make me too nervous when we went out riding. I was one of her horses that stayed with her at the Chateau de By. Of course, she had several other horses, but I was one of her favorites. I knew that by the way she brushed my whitish coat and took excellent overall care of me, her charming mare. I know that I have to step aside for a much bigger horse, a Percheron. She never owned one but she painted some especially her large and magnificent canvas of "The Horse Fair."

Let me talk myself about this particular adventure in painting. My name is Chevarot, a name that my master gave me as a work horse. Rosa Bonheur never knew me personally. She only knew me by my appearance at the horse fair when she entered the fair with her blue smock and her pants that she wore for fear of being recognized as a frail woman among so many men who would think that she did not belong there. I, a Percheron, am of the old tradition of work horses and my ancestors have been working the soil, carting logs, pulling huge loads and more. We were the prime draft horses. In Medieval times, we were used in battle by the knights. I'm sure that most of the legendary knights-errant had Percherons as their steed because we Percherons can boast of having Arabian blood, and we are strong and chivalrous, you might say. Someone has said that we, as a breed of horses, combine strength and attractiveness. That's why so many horse owners prefered the Percherons for their work and their delight in horse breeding. Percherons, I might add, are proud, alert, intelligent, and ever the willing workers. We have a large and fully prominent eye, a broad full forehead and straight face. We are very versatile, for we have the strength to pull heavy loads and the graceful style to pull a fine carriage. We even form four-in-hand teams to pull whatever load.

Now, as far as Rosa Bonheur is concerned, she admired us, the Perchertons, for both our beauty and strength as well as our stamina, as displayed in her great painting "The Horse Fair." Although she did not know me personally, she certainly appreciated my strong posture as a horse and my gleaming gray coat and mane shining in the sun's rays. I remember seeing her there looking at me intently, and wanting to get closer and closer, but the men would not allow her to do so. So, she sat on the side and began sketching me and the other horses along with the men handling us. She stayed there for hours and never seemed to get tired of it. She had a gleam in her eye that revealed her passion for horses. I could tell that she loved horses. She had to love horses to go to the police station to get a special permit to wear trousers in public just to be in the midst of men working at their slaughterhouse jobs. Then, she went to the slaughterhouse and to the horse fair just to be able to get the brute reality of it all, and then go to her atelier to continue sketching and finally paint this monstrous canvas that shows us, we the Percherons, as the animals of distinction and prowess. That's what I call it, the prowess of the Percheron. Like Senor Cervantes' tale of the mad knight, we Percherons are ready to tilt windmills if we have to and fight the good fight like the knights-errant of old. We are always ready to do whatever is asked of us. We are ever faithful and bold in our destinations and our vocation as Percherons. Yes, we do have a calling and that calling is to be at the service of men, men of labor, men of valor and chivalric tales, men of transportation, men of any kind of service. How about the ladies, you might ask. Well, we love the ladies, and we transport them to wherever they are destined to go, be it in town, in the countryside or on a leisurely ride in the park or any fantasyland they choose. You see, we are made to service the needs of all of you men and women.

Enough of this idle chatter, you beasts of burden and animals of leisure of Rosa Bonheur's menagerie. "Who says that?" "It is I, the Lord and Great Creator of the universe." "Oh, my God…it's God himself." "Yes, Rosa Bonheur. It's me and I have come to put a stop to this novel that not only delineates and describes the many paintings of yours but puts my creation into spheres that I did not create. Revenants of all things." "Yes, revenants because you created us with an imagination, not just an imagination that does not create but an imagination that can create all kinds of things such as revenants telling stories and talking to people here on earth, the readers." "I understand. I made people, men and women who turn out to be authors of books, hard cover books, soft cover books, e-books and so many other ways of printing and publishing that I could ever imagine from my own stance as Creator. I know that I'm supposed to know all things and be responsible for all things in such a way that I become your final judge at the end of Creation, but I have to take into consideration that I am God and that God can give or take away. I can take away all of your gifts and talents with the flip of my hand. Everything." "No, God, not everything, not our will, our independent will that you once said could never be taken away from us. We have a right to choose and make choices. We do make choices." "Yes, Rosa Bonheur, you do and they're good choices and not so good ones, and ultimately you are responsible for all of them." " I know that. When I get to heaven to finally meet you, I will have my baggage with me and you will judge me accordingly. For now, I am a revenant and so are all of those I have called forth as revenants under the magic spell of the author of this novel whose sense of creativity has given him the power to create as he so wishes with the talents you have given him in order to weave together a story of my life, my career and my influences in life, the influences that I have had and the influences that I made on people in my century and the centuries that followed and will follow until the end of time." " I have to agree with you on that. And, I give praise to the talent of this not very well known author of this novel that attempts to enlighten people's minds about creative talent at work in the world of the arts and all of the fine arts. I'm not sure if he has accomplished something worthwhile on the literary scene but I give him credit for attempting to broaden his own horizons while trying to write something of a certain value, the value of being creative as I am and will ever be That is why I allow human beings to imitate me and my creative sense." "Thank you, and thank you mister the author who was willing to risk his talent and even his skin to try and put together a work that took him hours and hours, energy and determination to succeed, and most of all, the research for the right word, the right sentence and the right alliance between fact and fiction. For a novel is not altogether fact, certainly not a documentary but a work woven together by the active and creative talent of one who knows and understands what it is to write and deliver a work of fiction, be it total fiction or partially fiction with threads of facts and personal experiences and the experiences of others." "Thank you Rosa Bonheur. By the way, what do you mean by risking my own skin?" "What I meant was that you would have lost yours if you had not done what you were inspired to do and did not succeed in doing it. I would have seen to it that your own skin would have been stripped from you, for that is how passionate I was about this work of yours." "Thank you for the inspiration and the marvelous works of art that you accomplished in your lifetime." "Let me tell you a little secret. I always knew you would write my story some day, and I realized it when you came to Fontainebleau recently and then tried to visit my Chateau de By, but the damn thing was closed. However, you persisted and managed to put things together and write this particular story based on my life and my career as an artist. I knew it all the time. Revenants know.You made me a revenant, and I know all of these things because you invented me that way." "That is what authors do, Rosa Bonheur. That is what authors do. They weave the magic of writing. If they're successful,well..." "One more thing." "What?" "I know you have me and Anna describe in the finest of details some of my precious paintings, but the reader has very little idea what they look like since there are no illustations in your novel, at least none proposed." " I know, and that may change. It depends on the publisher. However, the reader can certainly purchase a book of my paintings and match each painting that is described in my novel so that the reader can see for herself the splendor of your admirable craft as an *animalière*. A book of illustrations can do a whole lot for a reasder who has no illustrations at hand and wants to compare the words and descriptions with the actual painting. " "What a splendid idea. It would certainly be a worthwhile endeavor." "You see, I'm at your service the best I can, Madame Bonheur." "Yes, I can see. You assuredly have done a truly fascinating job of putting together facts and paintings with a touch of fiction, but imaginative and puposeful fiction, to add to your writing. I will recommmend you to the other authors here in the spheres." "That's very kind of you, but I am not of the same caliber as they are. They all wrote classics." "Maybe, just maybe, that someday some of your writings will become classics, or at least, attain the level of a touch of the classics. One never knows." "I know that my writings will never attain that level but I'm touched by your confidence in me." "We the revenants know more than you, and I say that the future looks bright for you and the many books that you will continue to write. Never consider yourself less than you are worth. I never did in my lifetime, for I considered myself worthy of being a good, if not an excellent, artist since I poured so much of myself into my art. Quality is predicated on the intensity of passion and determination." "I know." "Well, enough of this. I have to return to my sphere where I will look down on you and trust that you will ever put forth the very best of yourself as a person and as an artist, an artist with words. Artists are the gleam in God's eye. Did you know that?"

SILENCE. The grand and piercing silence of departure, and of the acknowledgement of love and beauty. "I Mozart, tell you to shout that to all the world for the world needs that right now. Proclaim and sing it out loud so that every soul hears it clearly and joyfully." "Shout what?" "That mystical silence." "But silence cannot be shouted." "Yes, it can. Try it." "How?" "By making it burst forth from your soul, that's how." "Oh!" "Yes, you have a soul, don't you?" "Yes, Herr Mozart. I have a soul, the soul of a writer who is mystified by all you geniuses of music, fine arts and words." "Now, keep it that way. I must go up to join my *confrères* up there in the sphere of composers and the sphere of the strains of music, for music soothes and delights the soul while replenishing it wherever it is." "Music of the night?" "No, music of the silence of the night."

SILENCE...the author is thinking.

He is thinking that he best thinks and creates in the silence of the most profound nighttime when the animals sleep their deepest sleep, the angels murmur songs of praise to the Almighty, the dead sleep their sleep of profound silence, people sleep in silence although they often are troubled in their sleep, and artists dream of their of their next work be it a painting, a novel or even a poem while a single line of a metaphor dangling in their silent but creative thoughts enriches their deep sleep waiting there like a lost sheep but recovered in the waking hours of the morning ready to be written down on paper. For the imagination and the creative mind never truly sleep. The author knows that. That is why he truly and sincerely believes in the Mozart effect. SILENCE GENERATES MUSIC. ..THE MYSTICAL MUSIC OF THE NIGHT...ever and ever still and generous with every heartbeat. The flesh may be weak but the spirit endures. Fly, my friends, fly to the stars and paint to your heart's content. Paint with the colors of light and creative genius that Rosa Bonheur had and continues to have for us, inspiring us to be creative and to love animals the way she did during her lifetime. A lifetime of passion and thrilling experiences of daring to do what the heart dares not do but the soul dares to surpass the heart's inabilities. That's why we creatures can fly over the nets of our inabilities and our failures. I as author, can truly fly and soar, at times, into he realm of the stars where a Bonheur, a Van Gogh or even a Mozart dared to go. "*La Nuit Étoilée*", "Starry, Starry Night" is proof of that. So is the "Magic Flute" and the soothing and loving eye of a lion like Fathma. I leave you, reader, with this thought, "Can a human being be as loving and carefree as a young mare prancing in the meadow?" Rosa Bonheur thought so. Only if the human being believes in the soul-filled personality of a horse. I know, I may sound a bit off-course and somewhat mad with the madness of a Van Gogh, a Mozart or even a Rosa Bonheur, but I must admit that I have been touched by the mystique of such artists to a point that I know that I can create with words and elicit joy on the part of the reader open to words and their spell. I NOW SURRENDER YOU AND MYSELF TO......S I L E N C E.

www.ingramcontent.com/pod-product-compliance
Lightning Source LLC
Chambersburg PA
CBHW050542190726
48284CB00003B/1177